"You might as well come in, I guess."

Though Cait's words were ungracious, her thoughts were anything but. Adam Webster *oozed* sex appeal.

He scanned her from head to toe, his gaze finally resting on her apron.

"Hmm, I didn't expect to be asked right off, but I'm willing if you are," he murmured as he wrapped his arms around her.

Cait stood still, stunned. There was no time to sort out the variety of sensations she was conscious of in his arms . . . before she began responding to his lips.

"Ah, Cait. Cait the cook," he whispered. "I somehow knew you'd taste like this."

"Wh-what *are* you doing?" she finally managed to gasp.

"Just following your instructions," he said. "I can read, you know." His gaze again traveled to her apron.

As she glanced down, Cait's outrage melted to mortification. Kiss the Cook! was emblazoned in bold black letters across her chest.

Roseanne Williams says a strange dream she had about five years ago may have altered her life's course. In the dream she and a friend visited a bookstore. They went straight to the romance fiction section, where Roseanne found books she authored; about six months later she began to write. Roseanne says *How Sweet It Is!*, her first published book, came about because "I love chocolate and I love to cook. And I've always wanted to write about a heroine who was atypical, who seemed real to me, so I wrote about Cait." Roseanne won the Romance Writers of America Golden Heart Award in the short, contemporary category for this book.

She lives in Portola Valley, California, with her husband and their cat, Milo.

How Sweet It Is!

ROSEANNE WILLIAMS

Harlequin Books

TORONTO • NEW YORK • LONDON
AMSTERDAM • PARIS • SYDNEY • HAMBURG
STOCKHOLM • ATHENS • TOKYO • MILAN

Published February 1989

ISBN 0-373-25337-0

Printed in U.S.A.

1

CAIT RAFFERTY HELD the long French chef's knife up to the bright television studio lights, drew a critical fingertip along the cutting edge and glanced at the three framed photographs propped up on the counter.

James Beard, rotund and genial, beamed back at her. Craig Claiborne grinned, circling thumb and forefinger together in approval. Julia Child, Cait's inspiration and chief guru, smiled back in unqualified encouragement. Cait could almost hear the cheery *"Bon appétit"* with which Julia concluded her televised appearances.

They were with her in spirit, if not in person, and if she had ever needed them, it was now. The three famous and fabulously talented chefs were just the lucky charms she needed to bolster her confidence, which sagged each time she thought of facing the TV camera's unfamiliar, unblinking eye.

"Five minutes to airtime," a production assistant called out from somewhere in the studio.

Cait took a deep breath and placed the knife on the hardwood countertop, lining it up with careful precision alongside a wire whisk, a chocolate grater and a long, shallow cake pan. If she was going to err, it would be on the side of caution, as usual. Julia, with her monumental reputation and unflappable stage presence, could afford to risk a fumble now and then. But Cait couldn't. Not yet.

Maybe she would be able to after her own cookbook hit the stands, she thought with a hopeful lift of her shoulders. Maybe then she could afford to drop a whole trussed chicken on the studio floor with Childlike aplomb. Maybe then she could afford to scoop it up with an amused chuckle, as it was reputed Julia once had, and plop it right back under the adoring noses of a TV audience of thousands.

Until that fortunate day it was plan, rehearse, plan and rehearse again for Cait. Yes, she'd wait until she was rich and famous before flipping *pots de crème* or *soufflés au chocolat* into her producer's lap. Dory Benjamin had enough to worry about as it was.

Dory had garnered her veteran's share of TV production awards, but *Northwest Live*, her new morning talk show, was up against a firmly entrenched local competitor on one channel and Phil Donahue on the other. Until the ratings proved the fledgling program's worth, Dory, Cait and everyone else on the set were keeping their collective fingers crossed.

Where had Dory gone anyway? Cait wondered. Her last glimpse of the petite older woman had been an hour earlier when Dory had rushed out muttering something about the worst always happening when you needed it least. Had the psychiatrist who was scheduled for the first segment failed to show? Cait squelched the thought. Disasters of that sort only happened in the movies, not on the premiere programs of new TV shows.

"Take your places for the intro, folks." The director's voice shook just a fraction on the command.

Cait's knees followed suit. Forgetting Dory, she bit her lip and scanned her recipe for the last time.

Eggs.

Sugar.

Butter.

Yikes! Butter. Had she melted it? Suddenly she couldn't remember. Panic chilled her insides and froze coherent thought for an instant. The list of ingredients blurred before her eyes as she stared down at it.

Butter . . . what was it about the butter?

She raised a clammy hand to her constricted throat. Good Lord. Was this *it*? Was this what she had shrugged off when Dory warned that live TV was different from the live cooking classes Cait taught for a living? Oh, dear heaven, was this stage fright, the dread affliction that sent even seasoned performers screaming to their psychoanalysts?

In that dumbstruck moment a square, tanned hand moved into the diminishing circle of her vision and turned the recipe around. She saw long tendons flex under burnished skin as supple fingers slid under the edge of the paper and lifted it. Unblinking, riveted to that masculine appendage, Cait's cinnamon-flecked gray eyes followed its ascent from the cutting board.

The next thing she was conscious of was blue. A blue like the Seattle sky. A blue like Lake Washington this crisp October morning. A sweat suit exactly like . . . exactly like . . . oh, what was it about that blue?

"Chocolate Ribbon Torte," the hand's owner read. "Looks like a first-class artery clogger if you ask me." The voice was mellow and as male as voices came.

Cait blinked and focused. Blue. That was it. The sweat suit in question was exactly like the one Doug had worn the day he walked out with his engagement ring. Except that on Doug the outfit looked like the exercise

gear it was. On this man, however, it looked positively—

"Tempting? Yes," he pronounced. "Healthy? No
way."

Cait's eyes rose from his hand to a hint of dark hair
at his open, ribbed collar. They lingered on the strong
throat that rose out of the collar and then lifted further
to the lips that had uttered those words of provocative
dissent. It was the way that mobile mouth quirked up
in a wide, teasing grin that spurred her out of her stage
fright and into a tardy but tart response.

"This 'artery clogger' just happens to be my spe-
cialty," she informed him, regaining her balance.

A heartbeat later she lost it again. Her gaze, on its
upward journey, tripped on his and fell headlong into
a pool of crystalline green.

He shrugged and leaned forward to rest his elbows
on her work counter. "Volunteering an honest opinion
seemed as good a way as any to get your undivided attention, and now that I've succeeded, I can't say I'm
sorry I did. Can you?"

"Three minutes!" the assistant called out.

"I certainly can," she said, summoning herself back
from the emerald enchantment of his gaze, the husky
timbre of his voice. She snatched her recipe back. "You
interrupt what I'm doing, imply that my torte is a death
threat and then ask if I'm sorry to find a...a health-nut
jock working on the same sound stage? I'm thrilled beyond words. *And* I'm rushed for time, so if you'd be
kind enough to move along..."

He did just the opposite. Raking a hand through his
thick dark hair, he moved around to Cait's side of the
counter. "A health-nut jock," he repeated with a dry

smile. "You're either an astute judge of people, or you're psychic. Which is it?"

"Neither. I've simply been blessed with an eye for the obvious," she told him, settling on him what she hoped was a cool look of dismissal. It wasn't easy to do since she'd just developed the most amazing weakness for green eyes and dark hair.

"So have I," he replied, letting this thick-lashed eyes peruse her up, down and up again.

Her lavender silk dress and burgundy half apron suddenly felt as wispy and insubstantial as a negligee. Loath to let him know it, though, Cait lifted her chin and replied, "It must be apparent to you, then, that I have far more pressing things to do than trade insults with stagehands."

"More pressing than telling just what else you've deduced about me?" he asked. "With a practiced eye like yours, there must be much, much more to tell."

In silent reply she forced herself to study him as he'd studied her. She let her gaze drop from his lopsided smile to the muscular wedge of his torso. Down from his slim hips to the whipcord length of his legs. All the way down to the worn pair of Nikes on his feet. No, her former fiancé had never looked quite like this in running gear.

"Well?" he prodded. "Care to fill me in on the obvious?"

"N-no." She gulped and turned back to her recipe.

"In that case," he said with a sigh, "I'll just have to join your little audience here until you change your mind, won't I?" He hefted himself up to sit on the counter next to Julia.

"Will you please get lost?"

He wagged a teasing finger. "Tell all and I will. Don't and I won't. It's up to you."

"Oh, all *right*, if that's what'll send you packing." Cait settled her hands on her hips. "First, you run. More than a few miles a day, rain, sleet or snow from the looks of those shoes."

"Go on." His mouth turned up at the corners in an amused grin.

"Second, I don't doubt you started the day with a scrumptious breakfast of yak cheese over roots and twigs with a few alfalfa sprouts for color. Organic, of course."

He chuckled. "I'm listening."

"Third, you analyze every bite you eat down to the last milligram of fearsome fat. Which is why you wouldn't be caught dead eating a piece of my delicious little dessert here, even on a bet. Right?"

He pursed his lips. "That depends. What would you be willing to bet?"

She folded her arms across her chest and tightened them a little. The things his eyes could do should be censored. His gaze was almost as palpable as a touch and just as disconcerting. Even more unsettling was this sudden desire of hers to welcome that green gaze. Oh, this was not like her at all. Would he never leave? Would he never stop looking at her in that way that made her blood both freeze and burn at the same time under her skin?

Answer the question and ignore the eyes, she told herself. What would she be willing to bet? Not what he seemed to be thinking she might wager. Just because other women probably said "yes" before he even asked didn't mean she intended to count herself among them.

He was immensely attractive, yes, but in all the wrong ways.

So what *would* she be willing to bet? Her glance fell on the high-tech food processor the studio supplied for her.

He looked taken aback. "That?"

"Why not?" she said, affecting her best poker face.

"Two minutes!" came the call.

"Hmm. Well, the French do make a fine machine," he said, disregarding the countdown.

"The best," Cait confirmed, wishing he looked a lot more discouraged and a little less interested.

He ran an appraising fingertip along the machine's streamlined white base. "This is yours?"

Cait watched that finger and felt her throat close in on itself. He might have been tracing the outline of a woman's body the way he was doing it ever so slowly. She had a sudden picture of that same touch exploring her own abundant curves instead of the spare, clean lines of the Cuisinart.

"No," she croaked out. She had to clear her throat before adding, "That one belongs to the station. Mine is at home."

She had to stop this. What was she doing, getting drawn in like this by a total stranger? Especially one who looked like the sort of man who never got "no" for an answer where women were concerned. Not that she couldn't see why. The eyes, the engaging smile, the way he— *Stop right there, Caitlin Mary Rafferty,* she told herself. *He reminds you too much of Doug, remember?*

"Rather hefty bet, isn't it?" he drawled, his eyes lighting up at her answer.

In an attempt to dim them she countered, "Not for someone who has more than a passing familiarity with your type." There was the heart of the matter, she reminded herself. She had no business forgetting how Doug had not only become a prime example of this man's type, but had also tried to mold her into a female version of it.

"You know," he murmured, "I'm beginning to think I'd like to have more than a passing familiarity with yours. How about having dinner with me tonight and I'll forget all about that bet."

He might also be the type to forget all about dinner in pursuit of other things once he got inside a woman's door, Cait thought. Complications like that she didn't need. It was time she stopped this one cold.

"How about letting me save you the time and expense?" she offered with a mock-helpful, mock-sweet smile. "For starters, chocolate is the mainstay of my diet. Second, whenever I feel the urge to break into a trot, I lie down until it passes. Finally, I like the extra few pounds I'm carrying around just fine, thank you."

"That means no?"

"Yes. Now, isn't it time you got back to adjusting your lights or sound or whatever it is you get paid to do around here?"

"I guess so. Whatever it is." He gave her a slow grin and pushed himself off the counter. "I'll be back, though."

"Whatever for?" she inquired in the driest tone she could manage.

"To collect on that bet."

"I'll save you the biggest piece, then," she promised, coating each word with patent disbelief. "Your arteries will never be the same, I assure you."

His grin widened. "Nonetheless, I'll be back, I assure you." With a taunting wink over his shoulder he turned and loped away.

Cait stared after him, positive he was bluffing. He had to be. Every lean, lithe line of that body shouted optimum health, maximum performance, vigilant maintenance. He ate to win. After Doug, she was an expert.

What she was less certain of was what had prompted his quite evident interest in her. Men like that, after all, went for the trim, athletic type. Evenly distributed over five feet six inches, her ample physical dimensions were just the opposite. It had to be just as apparent to him she ate no lean as it was to her he ate no fat.

Still, she couldn't quite suppress a regretful sigh when she thought of his eyes and smile. If only he weren't a health-nut jock. But he was. So wishing the opposite was fruitless. As compelling as the man might be, he was not her type, just as Doug no longer was.

At the thought of her ex-fiancé it occurred to her that Doug would never have sullied his peak-performance physique with a rich dessert just to snag a kitchen appliance on a bet. Neither, she told herself, would this Jack Sprat stagehand.

No, he wouldn't be back. Not with arteries as pristine as his probably were. She sighed again and turned her attention back to her recipe. Butter.

She racked her brain, then groaned when she spotted it on the electric burner. All that anxiety and it was right where she'd left it to melt on low heat.

"One minute!" The voice this time was Dory's.

Just calm down, Cait told herself. *Dory's back. The butter's melted. Everything's going to be just fine.* Sweeping the photos off the counter to the shelf underneath, she straightened to observe the last-minute activity in the studio.

The four cameras were aimed and waiting. Shirley Hutton, the program host, was seated in the conversation area adjusting her microphones. Off to one side the big clock ticked away.

"Thirty seconds."

Cait touched a finger to her lips. The petroleum jelly was still there where Dory had dabbed it over her lipstick. Dory knew all the tricks. There was, she thought gratefully, some comfort in knowing her lips wouldn't stick to her teeth in a permanent smile if her mouth went dry.

She fluffed her midlength auburn curls back from her face, smoothed the apron over her hourglass hips and wondered what had happened to the runner. He was nowhere in sight. All the better, she thought, remembering the effect his eyes, his smile, his undeniable sex appeal could have on a woman who might be susceptible to those masculine charms.

"Ten." The final countdown had started. "Nine. Eight. Seven." The assistant's voice lowered. "Six. Five. Four. Here . . . we . . . go."

Camera One's red light flashed on. Blond, blue-eyed Shirley flashed a cheerful smile of greeting, and *Northwest Live* was on the air.

"Good morning and welcome to *Northwest Live*," she announced to the invisible audience. "Today we'll visit with an author whose first book stayed on the nation's best-seller list for a phenomenal two years. He's a resident of Seattle now—Manhattan's loss, our gain. Next, an accomplished local chef will treat us to a delicious gourmet dessert from her new chocolate cookbook..."

Cait screwed her terrified face into a smile for Camera Two and breathed a shaky sigh when the red light went off a half second later.

"And last," Shirley wound up, "we'll watch a top beauty expert demonstrate a morning makeup routine that takes—believe it or not—four minutes. Stay tuned."

Cait watched the video monitor switch to a commercial before she stepped down from her side stage to join Dory behind the camera. Her legs felt like rubber. Worse, only seven mercilessly short minutes remained before she took her place in front of the camera again.

"Relax," Dory said with a reassuring smile.

"I'm trying," Cait said shakily. "What's the story with the lead segment, by the way? I thought it was a feel-good psychiatrist plugging her book."

Dory grinned. "It was. But that was before a truck tipped a load on the Evergreen Point Bridge and stopped traffic cold."

"She's stuck in traffic on the bridge? Now?" Cait squeaked.

Dory laughed and ran a hand through her close-cropped gray hair. "As far as we know, yes. Staying overnight with friends across the lake was her fool idea, not mine. I warned her that coming to the city over that bridge is a gamble even at the best of times."

"But . . . Dory, you don't sound the slightest bit upset. I don't get it."

"I'm not," Dory replied. "Of course they had to scrape me off the ceiling when I first heard. Things could have gotten grim, you know, with just a cook and a war paint expert and thirty long minutes to fill."

"'Grim' is too nice a word." Cait shivered. "So who's this big author you've got lined up?"

Dory peered at her in disbelief. "You didn't figure out from the intro who came to the rescue?"

Cait shook her head. "I'm new here, remember?"

"Sweet thing, didn't you hear what Shirley said?"

"Dory, I'm in the dark. Truly."

Dory rolled her eyes. "Honey, when was the last time you looked at a best-seller list?"

"The last time Julia Child was on one," Cait admitted with a sheepish smile. "I only read cookbooks and cookbooks."

"Ten seconds!" came the call.

"Believe me, sweetcakes," Dory whispered, "whatever you do or don't read, you've heard this famous name at least once in the twenty-six years you've lived on Planet Earth. Just watch."

"It seems like only yesterday," Shirley began, "that our first guest wrote the book that made publishing history. Over one hundred and fifty thousand copies of it sold in the first month alone. His second book sent total sales over the million mark. Now we hear he's suited up to write a third blockbuster. Adam Webster, author of *Runner's High* and *Second Wind*, come on out and say hello!"

Cait just sat and gaped, first at the book titles, then at the name and finally at the man who strode through a side door and onto the set.

He was suited up all right—in a sweat suit as blue as his eyes were green.

2

HER MOUTH AND EYES ROUND with astonishment, Cait watched the man she had bet against seat himself across from Shirley onstage.

Shirley asked the obligatory questions, and Adam answered them. Had she been quizzed, though, Cait couldn't have given even a hazy account of what was said at first. The discovery that he was who he was had catapulted her back four years in memory to one of the most painful periods of her life.

Runner's High. Webster's book had transformed Doug, her cuddly, paunchy, easygoing fiancé, into what could only be called an exercise addict. His appetite for her rich recipes and ripe physical proportions had declined with every mile he ran, every excess pound he shed.

Not content with reforming just himself, Doug had embarked on a fanatic crusade to deliver Cait, too, from the error of her ways. Cait, he decreed, would have to shape up.

She would first have to run. No woman in love ever ran harder or detested every sweaty, panting minute of it more than she did.

Next, Cait would have to eliminate sugar, salt and fat from her diet. She eliminated. Within hours life without chocolate loomed as almost a worse fate than life without Doug.

Come what may, Cait would have to lose weight. She lost. Who wouldn't after running her legs into the ground without a single Hershey's Kiss to ease the pain?

Fired with the missionary zeal of a convert, quoting Adam Webster chapter and verse, Doug preached the revelatory commandments that must be obeyed.

Thou shalt not ride when thou canst arrive by the sweat of thy brow alone.

Thou shalt not worship at the shrine of the Golden Arches nor that of the Thirty-One Flavors.

Pizza, pastries, peanut-butter-and-jelly sandwiches, all of it was *out*. There were more rules and regulations than there were calories in a pound of Belgian chocolates, and Cait staggered under the regimen. In all, she lost fifteen pounds she could easily spare and something else she couldn't. With those pounds went her own good opinion of herself.

The pain of remembrance tore through her now as she sat next to Dory and watched Shirley interview Adam. "There's more to running than you might think," Adam was saying. "The benefits aren't just physical, but emotional and psychological, as well— some even say spiritual."

Shirley looked totally convinced, but Cait's reaction was to roll her eyes in disdain. She, for one, had heard it all before in Doug's sermons. And look where it had gotten her then.

She closed her eyes, mentally plugged her ears against any further words of Webster wisdom and thought back to the good old days before Doug.

In the year before she met him, her self-esteem had undergone a positive transformation. Her victory was one she had achieved only with great effort. That she had to labor at it was testimony to a painful childhood spent as overweight, shy Caitlin Mary Rafferty.

Though the stresses and strains of adolescence eventually thinned her down to merely plump, graduation from high school found her still possessed of an inner image of herself quite at odds with the outer. In her mind's eye she was fat, not plump. Not even her loving, supportive parents could banish her mental picture of herself.

Then, during her sophomore year in college, she read an assigned book that declared fat a feminist issue. Reading it led her to take an objective look at herself nude in a full-length mirror. Her reflection there proved at least one of the author's contentions: twenty-five extra pounds didn't exactly make a woman a disaster area of a female.

So what if she could still be called heavy by some cultural and media standards? Who said she had to abide by them? For Cait, these were novel questions. The answers she came up with changed her life.

In time she was even able to tick off her good points with modest pride. She was healthy. She was a gifted journalism major. Furthermore, she was blessed with an offbeat sense of humor. Her auburn hair, gray eyes and quick, sincere smile offered nothing to complain of, either.

Of course, it hadn't happened overnight. Changing her inner picture of herself had involved setbacks as well as successes. Within a year, though, the setbacks formed a distinct minority.

In her junior year she met Doug and they were engaged. He was her first love, her first suitor, and he courted her with a sweet shyness that captured her virgin heart.

Now she sighed, shifted in the hard metal chair and opened her eyes. "Runners often write to me," Adam was telling Shirley, "that running has totally changed their lives."

Cait closed her eyes again. It had certainly changed hers. For the worse. At the beginning, though, she and Doug had been birds of a feather. No one was more appreciative than she that Doug's weight tipped the high side of ideal. Nor was anyone as sorry as Cait had been to see those pounds disappear when Doug got religion in the form of running.

Along with the pounds went the man Cait loved, the one man she'd rather split a Monster Combo pizza with than anyone else in the world. But pizza became a capital sin in Doug's reformed view of food.

And so it was that, after running a grueling five miles in a January rainstorm, Cait became an unrepentant sinner. It started in front of the mirror before she stepped into the shower. She stared at her reflection and saw a thin, cold, wet, hungry, miserable stranger. She didn't look like herself. She looked like Doug's idea of herself.

She stood in front of that mirror for a long time. When she had seen enough, she marched out of the bathroom and picked up the phone. Thirty minutes later she was tucking into her second slice of the biggest Monster Combo ever delivered by a pizza truck. Doug, when he walked in and found her sinning with a smile, was not as shocked as she'd expected.

It was Cait who wound up being shocked. A few days after she had returned to her wicked, wicked ways,

Doug dropped in to ask for his ring back. He'd actually been wanting to do it before, he said, but hadn't had the guts. It seemed he'd met someone else who jogged the same route he did. She was, he told Cait with obvious relish, a dead ringer for Jane Fonda from the neck down. It was beginning to feel like love at first sight for both of them, in fact. He was sorry, but figured it was better to end the engagement sooner than later.

Now Cait sat, ears and eyes closed to the man who'd written the first paragraph in the obituary of her first love. It was irrational, she knew, but she still held a grudge against Adam Webster for writing the book. In her mind, the end of her engagement and Adam Webster were inextricably linked.

"One minute to the commercial break and it's all yours, kid," Dory whispered. Cait's heart lurched. Her eyes flew open. She was next.

She glanced at the video monitor nearby. In no time she would be pictured there just as Adam Webster was now. Her hands went damp with perspiration as she gazed at his face. Though he wasn't classically handsome, Cait could see that he nonetheless possessed that indefinable something TV cameras fell in love with at first sight. She glanced around at the studio crew. Everyone was rapt with attention as Shirley wound up the segment with Adam. It was little wonder, Cait thought as she focused her attention on the man onstage.

When Mother Nature had designed Adam Webster, she had used all the right stuff. Dark hair, side parted as if by wind instead of comb. His fabulous eyes with their rim of thick lashes. The boyish, lopsided smile that made his square jaw and determined chin a surprise. Cait swallowed hard and dragged her gaze back to Shirley.

"If all this talk of working out has worked up your appetite, stay tuned," Shirley said to the camera. "Cait Rafferty's going to whip up something you and your devil of a sweet tooth won't be able to resist. We'll be back."

Cait pressed her clammy palms together and stood up. As she rose, it hit her. Good Lord. There was no way she could follow this polished act. The man was a knockout pro, calm, confident and assured. Half the population of Seattle was probably sprinting out right now to buy running gear. How could she, a complete greenhorn, follow this superstar exercise guru's class act? With dessert, of all things!

She sat back down, stricken. "Dory, I can't. This is too absurd. I mean, he says run it off before dinner, and I say put it back on with dessert?"

"Oh, brother." Dory clapped a hand to her forehead. "That never occurred to me when I phoned him in hysterics. I— Oh, jeez, Cait."

"Thirty seconds," someone called out.

"Well, it's too late now." Dory straightened in her chair and gripped Cait's arm with a firm hand. "You have to do it, sugarbear."

"But how? I can't—"

"Can't what?" Adam asked, sauntering up to them.

Cait sucked in a startled breath and stiffened. "Er, nothing, nothing. Dory was just, um, wishing me luck."

"Luck," Dory echoed. Her face brightened. "Right. Lotsa luck and knock 'em dead, sweetcakes."

"If *she* doesn't," Adam said, quirking an eyebrow, "that torte of hers will. Won't it . . . sweetcakes?"

Dory glanced from Adam to Cait. "You two have met?"

"After a fashion." Cait came to her feet, hands clenched in renewed indignation at her sides. "We've also bet, haven't we, Mr. Webster?"

"After a fashion," he murmured. "She's saving me the biggest piece."

Cait squared her shoulders, brushed past him and muttered, "Eat it today, wear it tomorrow."

"What on earth?" she heard Dory ask behind her. Adam made a reply Cait couldn't quite hear, then chuckled. *Let him laugh*, she thought as she stepped up to her work counter. Absurd as it might be, she'd follow class with calories and hold her own.

"Ten seconds," the director warned.

Cait braced herself behind the counter and glanced over at Adam. He was sprawled in the chair she'd just vacated, directing at her a green gaze that held a taunting challenge. She lifted her chin and looked away. She'd show him. So what if he had class, confidence and charisma? Here at her fingertips she had something that could compete with the best. She had Chocolate, with a capital C.

It was a noble thought, one Cait held firmly in mind as the director signaled Shirley to begin. "Our next guest," Shirley announced, "is known to you from the *Cait's Cookin'* spot on a local radio station. You'll also be happy to hear that her first cookbook, *Chocolate à la Carte*, will soon be published by Singleton House. Cait, what's cookin' over there?"

"Chocolate," Cait replied, looking the dreaded camera straight in the eye. "If you're addicted to that marvelous stuff like I am, you'll love Chocolate Ribbon Torte. It's a real cinch to make, as you'll see."

Demonstrating as she talked, Cait whipped up a chocolate batter for the flat sheet cake that was the basis of the torte. From the oven she drew out an already baked and cooled version of the same thing. All the while she could feel those green eyes on her, intent and unwavering.

She would *not* let him get to her, she vowed. Her many hours of preparation were paying off too handsomely for her to stumble now. Everything was going like clockwork, her delivery smooth, her movements deft and sure.

Explaining each step, she blended eggs, cream and white chocolate into a snowy mousse and spread it over the entire surface of the cake. That done, she sliced it lengthwise in two-inch-wide strips with her big knife.

Out of the corner of her eye she saw a smile play about Adam's lips. Amusement, no doubt, at the way her cheeks were growing hotter by the second under his seductive stare. There was no other word for the subliminal messages his eyes were sending her way. Once again she felt her insides go liquid in response.

"Now, you're ready to begin shaping the torte," she told the camera as her heart skipped beats in her chest. "First roll up a strip and place it cut side up in the middle of your cake plate. Then coil each remaining strip around in a continuous circle. You should end up with a two-inch-high cake resembling a huge slice of a jelly roll."

If only she could scowl at him and stop this stage-set seduction. If only. As it was, though, she had to smile sweetly and say, "To finish it off in style, you'll need six jumbo maraschino cherries and a wide red satin ribbon. Just cluster the cherries in the center, stems up. Then wind the ribbon around the circumference, tie the ends in a big bow and there you have it—Chocolate Ribbon Torte."

Her timing was perfect. The camera zoomed in for a close-up and then clicked off, ending her maiden voyage on the seas of daytime TV. Though almost limp with relief, she managed a victorious glance at Adam before stepping down from the set and turning her back on him.

Hands clenched in frustration at her sides, she headed for the ladies' room. Not until the show was over and Adam Webster gone for good did she intend to come out.

HOURS LATER Cait let herself into her small duplex apartment and collapsed in the nearest armchair. What a day! First, *Northwest Live*; then, the two cooking classes a downtown department store paid her to teach in its gourmet kitchenware shop; last, a series of hectic errands in city traffic.

Scrunching down into the cushions, she closed her weary eyes. With a welcoming "meow" her cat, Truffles, leaped from the couch into Cait's lap. There, her sleek pet curled up and began the rhythmic purring and kneading that signified utter feline bliss.

The slow, measured stroking of Truffles's glossy, cocoa-brown fur usually relaxed Cait as little else could.

This daily ritual of theirs was a meditation of sorts, quiet time that calmed both Cait and the cat.

Today, though, it failed to work its usual wind-down magic. Already Cait's thoughts were seeing to that. Free of any immediate concerns, they made an unerring U-turn to what had happened that morning after she emerged from the studio rest room.

Behind her closed eyes a mental videotape of the scene played itself out in vivid color and sound. There she was, passing out paper plates and plastic forks to Dory and the crew amid a noisy chorus of congratulations. One camera operator praised her polished performance, the other her cool poise.

"Tell me I don't know a star when I see one," Dory boasted to one and all. "Julia Child, watch out!"

Adam Webster, Cait noticed, was conspicuously absent. All talk and no action. The Jack Sprat in him had won the bet for her. She smiled to herself and poised her knife over the torte to make the first cut.

"I feel like a bride without the groom," she quipped with a slaphappy grin.

A second later it froze in place on her lips as a hand covered hers from behind. After craning her neck, she squeezed her eyes shut against the color they encountered. Blue.

"Allow me," Adam murmured, and with a killing smile played the groom to her bride in the cutting of the cake.

"Three cheers for the man who saved the day," Dory crowed. "Our hero, Adam Webster!"

Everyone cheered and waved their paper plates high at their hero—all except Cait. Adam was pressed so close against her she couldn't even think, much less move. Worse, that closeness was playing immediate havoc with more physical senses than she'd known she had.

She could feel the warmth of his body through her dress. He felt so solid behind her, so male, so— Damn him, he had no right to be butting in like this on her moment of glory. But extricating her hand from his very firm grip required more muscle than Cait possessed right then.

"Relax," he whispered and pressed closer as he guided her hand and the knife in slicing the entire torte.

Only when the task was complete did he release her and step away. Cait swayed on unsteady legs, disoriented for an instant. All around everyone was oohing and aahing in anticipation over the torte. She barely heard them above the roar of blood in her ears.

"Dish it up, Cait," she heard someone say as if from very far away.

She shook her head to clear it. "What?"

Pointing to the knife in Cait's hand, Dory commanded, "Serve, girl. Now," and held out her plate.

"Oh." Cait came back to herself in one big rush. "Oh! Sure. You bet." Blushing furiously, she served Dory first, then passed a huge slice to Adam and the rest to the others. Within seconds there was much stuffing of faces and smacking of lips.

"Scrumptious, Cait."

"Dee-lish, sweetcakes."

"Heaven, sheer heaven."

Cait glanced at Adam and caught him looking down at his hefty slice with a decidedly peculiar expression on his face. When he caught her looking at him, though, he switched to a cocky grin. Lifting his fork, he saluted her with it and proceeded to carry through on his promise. Bite by bite, one deliberate forkful after another, he downed the whole piece, cherry and all.

Cait stirred now in her armchair. Never, she thought, would she forget the tip of his tongue as it flicked to the corner of his mouth to capture the tiny, final victory of the last crumb. Nor would she ever forget how his eyes had remained on her the entire time.

Most of all, she'd never forget how he'd strolled up to her after the others had dispersed and said, "I can drop by to collect the spoils whenever it's convenient. How about tonight around seven?"

What else could she do but reply, "Fine. The receptionist out front can give you the address."

He grinned. "I already got it from Dory—address, phone, marital status."

"That last vital statistic," she bristled, "is none of your business. Furthermore, Dory has no right to—"

"Dory's words exactly," he cut in. "She backed down when I reminded her she owed me one for doing the show today instead of next week as we had earlier planned."

"Oh."

"See you at seven."

"SEVEN," CAIT REPEATED aloud now into the silence in her living room. She opened her eyes and focused on the mantel clock. It was already five.

In two hours the man she had once loved to hate would knock on her door. She would be forced to invite him into her living room with its eclectic mix of second-generation antiques and secondhand modern. Here he would stand, Doug's hero.

"Stow it, Cait," she warned herself. A bittersweet stroll down memory lane would serve no purpose now. Four years had, after all, healed her wounds. They had, in addition, put her where she was today.

Now, at last, she had realized her secret dream of stepping up from cooking classes and a radio spot to TV. Not bad for Caitlin Mary Rafferty, former chubbette, shrinking violet, perennial high school wallflower.

Buoyed by the day's success, she scooted Truffles out of her lap and headed for the kitchen. If Wednesday's recipe was to equal today's—and Friday's to rival Wednesday's—she had to get cooking. Dory had guaranteed her three appearances each week for one month to prove her worth as a cook to the sponsors.

In the kitchen doorway she halted and heaved a sigh. Crammed with the tools of her trade, her tiny cubicle of a kitchen hardly resembled the grand workplace of a TV chef. The sight of it was sufficient to take most of the wind out of her sails.

She sighed again. She might have come a long way from wallflower, but she was still renting a cramped apartment and barely earning a living. The financial risk she had incurred by quitting the paper to teach classes hadn't quite paid off yet. There would be no fancy kitchens for her, in fact, unless the book took off.

Snatching an apron from the many she kept on a row of kitchen hooks, she tied it on, lost in her favorite daydream. Oh, what she wouldn't give for a big fancy kitchen like the one Julia Child used on TV. And, oh, what she wouldn't give for the army of kitchen gadgets Julia probably owned. Child was one cook who wouldn't suffer by losing an impulsive bet like the one

Cait had lost today. Impulse. How unlike her to act on it.

But Cait had, and now the very thought of that man using her one and only Cuisinart to whip up wheat germ smoothies or tofu soufflés was positively nauseating. Cait could only hope the chocolate torte mucking up his lily-white arteries today was having the same effect on him.

Up to her elbows in sifted flour two hours later, she groaned at the sound of the doorbell. Before answering it, she darted a quick peek into the oven where Wednesday's recipe was baking away. The sweet little rounds were browning nicely, though a little too fast. A scant minute or two more and they would be done.

Making a mental note of it, she sped out of the kitchen, berating her unwelcome visitor under her breath. Though she was willing to concede he wasn't *personally* responsible for her breakup with Doug, he *was* responsible for unfairly winning the bet.

Any millionaire author who would resort to his tactics to win a trivial kitchen appliance from a small-time cook had to have an overinflated opinion of himself. As far as Cait was concerned, that was enough. Adam Webster, for all his sex appeal, remained a card-carrying leader of the opposition.

Framed in the open doorway, though, he looked not at all petty, selfish or egotistical. Dressed in jeans and a sweater, he looked like nothing so much as an ordinary man.

Well, "ordinary" wasn't quite the word, she had to amend hastily. He was, after all, the man whose appearance on *Northwest Live* today had set the station's

phones ringing for hours afterward. According to
Dory, the female callers outnumbered the men three to
one. No, anyone who looked that male, that aware of
it and that comfortable with the fact wasn't your
everyday Joe.

In testament to it, his faded blue denims outlined in
more specific terms what the sweat suit had skimmed
so casually that morning. Slim, hard hips rode on long-
muscled thighs that tapered to lithe calves and Loaf-
ered feet. The rough-knit black wool sweater he wore
deepened even further the shadows in his dark, wind-
blown hair.

With a sweeping glance that locked Cait's breath in
her throat once again, Adam scanned her from head to
toe. Down her face his eyes moved, down the front of
her apron to her heeled pumps and back up to the apron
again. There they remained fixed for a suspended moment.

Whatever it was that made his lips curve into that
sudden smile mystified her. It was the same smile that
had so undone her at first sight that morning. And the
same one he'd worn as he forked his way through the
torte to victory.

All in all, it was hardly the reaction she had expected
to "the Pillsbury Doughgirl" she was certain she resembled at the moment. Frowning, she motioned him
in.

"Hmm, I didn't expect to be asked right off, but I'm
ready and willing if you are," he murmured in the moment it took him to step inside and wrap his arms
around her.

In the first few seconds of that sudden embrace, Cait
stood still, stunned. By the time she regained a vestige

of her voice, her startled protest was dammed in her throat by Adam's lips covering hers.

Her flour-dusted hands curled into fists to ward him off. But as the warmth of his mouth met and mingled with hers, she felt them go slack and flatten against his chest.

There was no time to sort out the variety of sensations she was conscious of in his arms. His seeking lips on hers, his hands curved into the small of her back, the smooth muscles of his chest pressed against her breasts—each separate thing vied with another, sending rational thought right out the open door.

"Ah, Cait. Cait the Cook," he whispered. "I somehow knew you'd taste like this."

Each whispered word moved his mouth against hers and sent her heart into a chaos of irregular pulses.

"Wh-what *are* you doing?" she said with a gasp, stifling an impulse to step closer into his arms as the chill night air blew in the door.

"Just following your instructions," he breathed.

She forced her head back from his. "Are you out of your mind? I never—"

"Not in the slightest," he interrupted. "I have all my wits at hand, and believe me, I can read as well as the next man."

Read what? her jumbled mind asked as he coaxed her mouth into meeting his once more. But there was no way to form an audible question, for his breath was stealing hers, spiriting away her power to speak or think clearly.

Most unnerving of all was the response he evoked from her with the velvet touch of his lips, his hands that slipped down the length of her back and up again. It made not a shred of sense that she should react to this man's presumptive kiss by kissing him back. Nevertheless, she was doing just that.

None of it made any sense. She only knew that everything was a beguilement right then, from the strong thighs fused to hers to the masculine scent that tempted her nostrils with a hint of musk. No, not musk, she decided in a daze. It was something darker, duskier.

"Is that you going up in smoke, or is it me?" he mumbled, his lips never losing contact with hers.

Smoke. Was that the dark, dusky something in the air? The word stole further into her hazy consciousness and then billowed up, a very real threat. What was going up in smoke was more than the dry tinder of her self-control.

It was the Double Dutch Chocolate-Chocolate Chunk Cookies in the oven!

Perceiving the situation at the same time, Cait and Adam tore apart to leap in unison toward the kitchen.

"Now we know why that guy calls himself the Galloping Gourmet," Adam cracked, crossing the finish line three strides ahead of her to grab a pot holder.

"Burned! All of them burned alive!" Cait gasped, skidding to a stop as he flung the oven door wide and pulled out the smoking cookie sheet.

Sallying past her with the incinerated remains, Adam set the pan outside on the front step. Shaking his head, he walked back inside.

"If that was dinner," he said, lobbing the pot holder to her; "you're out of luck. Looks like I'll just have to take you out for a bite to eat, after all."

Cait snatched the quilted square out of the air. "That was not dinner," she corrected, "and you will not take me out for a bite of anything. You can't walk in and assault me one minute and waltz me out to dinner the next."

"Assault?" he repeated. He returned his gaze to her apron front. "Accepting an open invitation doesn't add up to assault."

Her outraged gaze followed his and melted to mortification at what she saw. From the jumble of aprons she owned, she had pulled out one sporting a printed slogan without taking the slightest notice of it.

Kiss the Cook! it said. In bold black on raging red.

Cait squeezed her eyes shut, helpless to contradict the fact. Of all the slogans on all the aprons on all the overflowing hooks on the wall, her unwitting hand had selected the only one capable of inviting the very thing Adam had done.

Added to that, she looked a downright mess. Red-and-black apron, lavender dress and mealy white hands to set the whole thing off. What style. What flair.

She couldn't have looked more ridiculous if she had tried. She looked about as stylishly turned out as a circus clown. Furthermore, the printed command on her apron was about as subtle as a billboard. Acutely aware of it, Cait reacted in the only way possible short of humiliated tears.

Giddy, irrepressible, a giggle bubbled up in her and spilled into a peal of laughter. The spectacle of Adam's black sweater streaked with flour from her hands made the whole thing even more of a joke.

As tears of mirth began to sparkle in her eyes, a corner of Adam's expressive mouth twitched. Then the other followed, and with a rich rumble of a belly laugh, he threw his handsome head back and joined in.

They were both well on their way to whoops and howls when the phone in the kitchen rang. Arms wrapped around her aching sides, Cait ran to answer it.

"Hi, Cait. It's me."

It was Jeremy Ainsley calling from New York. No longer did it seem strange to Cait that all she knew of him was his voice. After countless long-distance conversations she had grown used to the fact that an editor could guide a cookbook through the entire publishing process without once conferring with the author face-to-face.

"Jeremy! Wha-what's up?" Cait choked out.

"Cait, are you all right?"

"Just give me a sec."

"Hey, you sound like— You're not crying, are you?"

"No," she told him, pulling herself into line at last. "Just the opposite, actually."

"Ah, tears of laughter," he said. "I'm in luck."

Cait sobered up completely at that. "Somehow it doesn't sound as if *I* am. What's the bad news, Jer?"

"How about the good news first?" he hastened. "Your second manuscript looks great. Just a few revisions and a format change and it's complete. Easy money."

"I already know that," Cait declared. "You sent me the revisions last week."

Jeremy cleared his throat. "Er, yes, well. Thing is, I called to tell you the publication schedule on *Chocolate à la Carte* might get pushed back a little more. Possibly a month or so."

Cait slumped against the refrigerator door and groaned. This was the second time Jeremy had called to announce a delay. Now it would be that much longer before the royalties started flowing in, if they ever *did* start. That much longer to scrimp and scrape for the payments on the new word processor and the used car. Oh, why had she thrown caution to the winds and spent the advance checks right away?

"Cait?" Jeremy ventured into the silence. "Are we still friends?"

"That's what I asked my landlord the last time the rent was overdue, Jeremy."

"Hey, tell him it's going to be a blockbuster. Worth waiting for every penny, mark my words."

"That's the story I've been giving the bank for the past six months," she wailed and then wished she hadn't. She'd forgotten Adam was there. Sure enough, he appeared in the kitchen doorway, his smile fading from his lips, his eyes clouding with concern.

In the cradle of his arms Truffles purred sweet contentment. The little traitor. Over the cat's adoring head Adam's clouded gaze remained fixed on Cait.

"How's the next book coming along?" Jeremy said, eagerness to change the subject apparent in his voice.

Cait couldn't frame a reply for a moment. Her third book, still just an idea, was the furthest thing from her mind right then. Instead, her attention was riveted on the paradoxical fire that flared in the sea-green depths of Adam's eyes, so like the sudden flame in the cool heart of an opal.

One of those fascinating quirks of nature, the phenomenon tantalized and invited a second glance, a closer scrutiny. Cait took a tremulous breath and reminded herself that yielding to temptation of that sort was not something she could risk with this man. Not after the cutting of the cake in the studio when he'd fired her blood with a touch. Not after that kiss at her door.

Lips still warm with the memory of it, she focused on the safety of the calendar next to the phone and told Jeremy, "It's still on the back burner, but I'll get a proposal to my agent by the end of the month."

"The sooner the better. And sooner is better if you can manage it, Cait."

Out of the corner of her eye Cait saw Adam vacate the doorway, leaving her alone again but not out of earshot. Her place was too small to afford anyone in it the luxury of privacy. Cait pulled her attention back to her editor. "These days I only have time to juggle the rent and car payments."

"You sound just like your agent," he complained. "Those were her words exactly. Both of you on my case at the same time is just what I need."

Cait had to laugh. "Looks like you're stuck with both of us, Jeremy."

"Have a heart, Cait." He sighed. "Give a poor guy a break."

"Listen, Jer. With my soft head for business I *need* an agent who can plead my case. You know that. I could also use a creative accountant, a fearless financial adviser and a landlord with the patience of Job. Any leads?"

"When the book hits the stands, they'll beat a path to your door for your autograph," he said. "It's just a matter of time. And speaking of that rare commodity, how about staying home every once in a while? Then this overworked, underpaid editor could call you during office hours."

"When I'm a published author, holding my published book in my hot little hand, I will," she scolded back.

"Touché." He chuckled. "Night, Cait."

She hung up the phone and glared at the calendar. Another month or so. An eternity.

"Mmm. That feels good, doesn't it? Mmm, yes. You're a real beauty, aren't you?"

Adam's voice coming from her living room was soft, gentle, filled with tenderness. Shelving her financial woes for a second, Cait just stood there and listened to the soothing sound.

"Do you like to be scratched under your chin, hmm? Do you?" he crooned.

In her mind's eye Cait could see Truffles lifting her chin to his caressing fingertips, arching her back to the sweep of his hand. So the man had a way with cats.

The same way he had with women? Just thinking about the proof he had already given of *that* sent a delicious shiver of remembrance down Cait's spine. She enjoyed the sensation for a moment and then shook it off. This was no time to forget that he had been irritating beyond belief and beat her at her own game. Just because he could kiss so thoroughly she could still feel it was no reason to forget that.

It was impossible, though, not to be captivated by the sound of his voice. He sounded so sweet, so safe, so reasonable. So different from the man who had taken her in his arms a few minutes ago.

The man who had done that was unpredictable, impulsive, someone who stirred feelings in her no man ever had. Still, the soft timbre of his voice now was so compelling she felt a momentary desire for the ability to purr as Truffles was surely doing.

In truth, she felt almost afraid to move out of the haven of her kitchen. Nothing in her experience had prepared her to deal with Adam Webster. Yet here he was, settled in her living room making an abject slave of her cat.

Cats and women. He did seem to have a way with both. A way she couldn't afford to succumb to a second time. Trouble was, she couldn't help wondering what it would be like to do just that. That way he had about him was beginning to get under her skin.

It was frightening, and more than mildly stimulating. She drummed her fingers in a flustered tattoo on the countertop. What was she going to do with this charming male who was her opposite in so many ways and her undoing in more than one?

Maybe she *should* let him take her out to dinner. Then again, maybe not. One date might lead to another, and she had no intention of getting involved with another Jack Sprat. Staying on her own turf, however, held no guarantee of safety. Witness what had happened the instant Adam walked in the door.

Whatever she did, she knew she had to extinguish the inexplicable attraction growing between them before things got out of hand. Dinner. Should she or shouldn't she? And where would they go? Most likely a salad bar if she had him pegged right.

She grimaced. Lettuce. It was the last of the four food groups she'd choose for dinner. If anything, she'd choose . . . Her fingers drummed to a stop. Now there was a thought. Dinner at the place of her choice just

might do
liant.

Dinner at the
would be argumen
acquainted. Adam see
that score. Cait, howev
four years before was amp
a mismatch.

Her eyes sought out the frame
above her stove as a reminder. Of
Love, it read, the First is Sweeter by Far.
remembering in the light of that kiss. A few
sort Adam was capable of administering m
her to let more than an ovenful of cookies g
smoke.

Yes, she would do well to heed the proverb, remem
ber the lesson she had learned and retain chocolate as
her one and only. Pound for pound, it was safer and far
more predictable than Adam Webster. Having decided
that, she walked out of the kitchen.

"Adam," she announced, "I've given it some thought
and I'll take you up on dinner after all. I know just the
place."

He lifted a speculative eyebrow. "I've been doing
some thinking of my own," he replied, "and if you don't
remove that apron really fast, I can't promise we'll ever
get there."

the trick. On second thought, it was bril-

restaurant that had just come to mind
t enough against their getting better
med to need some convincing on
r, did not. Her experience of
e proof of the folly of such

d proverb she'd hung
ine Chocolate and
Each word bore
r more of the
ght tempt
up in

...tested its keen blade with a graceful fingertip. Then he'd let the breath out in a slow, silent whistle as her movements arched her spine in a curve and lifted her full breasts into provocative relief beneath the lavender silk of her dress.

Nude, he'd thought at the time, she could have posed for one of the Renoir bathing scenes he'd seen at the Louvre on his last European book tour. Or did she more resemble a slightly scaled down Gibson Girl? Maybe so. Or perhaps a full-bodied Devonshire milkmaid, with her fair skin and gray eyes. Whatever the case, he had decided then, she was as easy on the educated male eye as a woman of her height, weight and liberal proportions had ever been in past eras.

There was nothing subtle or subdued in her rich curves. One thing he was quite sure of—he'd never wake in the dark of the night with *her* in his bed and not know who she was by touch alone.

Now, as Cait swung her long, shapely legs up into the van, he was moved again to fantasies of waking in the dark of the night with her. It was a thought as provocative as the thought of making love to her at midnight. So much so that he had to rein in a brash impulse to lure her back into her apartment on some pretext or other.

"That's the way the cookies crumble sometimes, Webster," he muttered after he shut the van door on the sight of Cait's faintly dimpled knees. "Maybe they'll crumble your way next time."

The problem was, he couldn't be certain there would be a next time for him with Cait Rafferty. She had the look and manner of a woman who'd made up her mind against something. That something, he sensed, was him. It was refreshing, in a way, and more than attractive to a man who welcomed a romantic challenge and rarely found it. Lord knows it felt good to be the one in pursuit for a change.

He circled the van, slid into his seat and started the engine. "Where to?" he asked.

"Four blocks straight ahead and four to the left and we're there," she replied.

"That's all?"

"All?"

He switched the engine off. "We could walk that distance in a matter of minutes."

"Speak for yourself, Adam. I never walk if I can ride, thank you."

"Eight blocks isn't exactly an Olympic marathon," he observed dryly.

"That may be, but it's not my idea of a cheery little stroll, either." She settled back and snapped her seat belt shut.

Adam studied the determined set of her chin. It seemed impossible now that she was the same woman who had warmed and softened to his kiss. Or the same woman who had erupted into deep, rich laughter just minutes ago. He couldn't, however, forget that she had. Nor could he forget what a pleasure it had been to join in and laugh with her.

Most of all, he couldn't deny how much he wanted to laugh with her again. And kiss her again. And numerous other things. As he looked at her, he decided he would go for at least another kiss before the night was out. Whatever it took, the fixed line of her lips would melt to softness under his again. If there was one thing he knew, it was how to go the distance.

"Okay, we'll ride, then." He clamped his jaw down into a squared imitation of hers, started the van and pulled into the early-evening traffic.

An awkward, suspended silence stretched between them before Cait broke it by volunteering a halfhearted explanation. "It's not that I have anything against exercise in theory," she told him. "I just have a lot against it in practice. I'm not the athletic type."

"You don't have to be to walk eight blocks," he countered. "Try it sometime. You might just like it."

"I have," she replied, "and I didn't."

"I see."

"I don't think you do."

"Have it your way, then. As for me, I'm one of those guys who can't live without it."

Cait heard a subtle shift in his voice as he said that and glanced over at him. His eyes were steady on the road, but his knuckles looked almost white as his hands gripped the steering wheel. Did he mean he was as addicted to running as Doug had been? If he couldn't live without it, he must be. This was some night she had ahead of her.

"Well, I can't live without chocolate, so we're probably even," she granted him. "Even if our waistlines aren't."

"Yours looks all right to me," he said without taking his eyes from the road.

"That's very gentlemanly of you, but I know that Jane Fonda I'm not."

"I'm not being a 'gentleman' about it," he replied. "I've figured out that you're not Jane and never will be at the rate you're going."

Unprepared for such a candid response, Cait couldn't help bristling a little. "What's that supposed to mean— exactly?"

"It means I agree you'll never win an Oscar for best actress in a leading role unless you switch professions fast."

Cait blinked in complete surprise and sputtered, "I . . . I wasn't referring to her Oscars."

"Oh? Well, if it's age you're referring to, I agree with you there, too. She's decades older than you are, no question about it."

Stymied into momentary silence, Cait darted a baffled sidelong glance his way. He was smiling, his eyes on the road, his hands now relaxed on the steering wheel. The smile, Cait could see, was not one of amusement. Nor was there even a hint of smugness there. More than anything it was a perceptive, understanding smile. He knew what she meant.

He had tact, she couldn't help thinking, and grace. The defensive line of her lips softened and trembled into an upward curve. So he wasn't the egotist fame and fortune might have created. Not entirely.

Then, remembering why she was with him, where they were headed and for what purpose, she frowned. Sensitive and tactful though he might be, she must guard against going all soft and mushy over this man at the first positive sign.

"Age isn't the issue, as you well know," she retorted, deepening her frown with some effort.

"All I know is we're going to need a parking space any minute now," he replied. "Keep an eye out for one, will you?"

"We're here already?" She looked out to find that they had, indeed, arrived at the destined intersection.

Adam shot a droll glance at her. "Time flies when you're having fun."

Time did, Cait had to admit, have a way of winging by when Adam was around. Witty, discreet and perceptive, he could never be termed a bore.

A tiny dart of conscience pricked her as she peered through the windshield in search of an empty space. If he was less a selfish egotist than she had earlier thought, were there other things he wasn't, as well? Considering what she had in store for him tonight, she hoped not.

A movement at the curb diverted her from the disturbing thought. "There!" She pointed ahead. "There's one just ahead—perfect."

As Adam maneuvered the van into the tight space, Cait wondered, as she had wondered from the moment she saw it, why he drove the aging rattletrap. Could it be that he was also unassuming and unpretentious beneath that superstar exterior? Or was the van merely evidence of reverse snobbery? "Millionaire author's head isn't turned by success"—that sort of thing.

Adam cut the engine and turned to Cait. "So, where's this place we're dining tonight?"

"There." Cait pointed ahead to the modern facade of one of Seattle's finest hotels.

Adam's face fell. "A hotel?"

"Why not? You have something against them?"

"Too many years of checking in and out of them on too regular a basis," he said with a sigh. "Not to mention one too many cases of indigestion along the way."

"But I know the kitchen staff here. They do truly marvelous things with the, uh, the freshest of ingredients." Having executed that carefully worded statement, Cait had to endure yet another tiny prick of doubt about having chosen to take Adam there. If only he hadn't dispatched the Fonda issue with such charm. If only he drove a Rolls-Royce or a Maserati.

If only he wouldn't look at her as he was looking at her now. The expression in his eyes as he gazed into hers was guileless, open, searching. No man, she found herself thinking, could look at a woman like that and not be the soul of sincerity.

"Really fresh?" he inquired in a husky murmur.

She nodded and swallowed hard. Dark-fringed jade, his eyes searched her face and deepened to sea-green. Deep inside herself, Cait felt something give way. Oh,

Lord, he could look at a woman like no man she had ever encountered in her life.

"Okay," he yielded in the same husky tone. "You're the cooking expert, after all."

She nodded again, mind arrested in midthought, words halted in midthroat, able only to sit and gaze back at him. Time, then, seemed to slow to a crawl as Adam clicked his seat belt free with one hand and leaned toward her. His other hand caught her chin and turned her face toward his. Twisting over the gearshift, he gently placed his mouth on hers.

Cait's numbed brain considered stopping him, but only for an instant. As she breathed in his clean scent, felt the warmth of his breath on her lips, the thought vanished.

"Ahhh, Cait," he breathed, moving his parted lips in an inviting circular motion on hers, "kiss me, Cait."

In the far recesses of her mind she was aware they were parked on a public street. People strolled by on the sidewalk. None of it fully registered, though. Only the hot press of his mouth against hers, only the soft dart of his tongue against hers, registered at that moment.

A slight moan sounded deep in his throat as she opened to him, tasted him, strained sideways against her seat belt to deepen the contact. He tasted so good she couldn't resist it. Nothing had ever tasted as heavenly in her whole life. Nor had anything felt as divine as the stroke of his fingers down the arched column of her throat.

"Sweet..." Adam murmured into her mouth, "...so sweet."

Down from the hollow at her throat his fingers drifted, down to the soft swell of her right breast.

Curving his palm to her, he brushed the pad of his thumb over the crest.

Cait gasped as her nipple gathered in a bud of exquisite sensation at his touch. His was a man's touch, knowing and sure. A touch that sent streamers of desire from secret place to secret place in her body.

"Adam," she choked out.

He lifted his head but not his hand. "Cait, I—"

She shook her head. "Don't."

Slowly, reluctantly, he withdrew his hand and settled back into his seat. "I'm sorry," he murmured with a frustrated sigh. "Really."

"Me, too," she mumbled with a wary glance over at him. What she saw was surprising. He did look genuinely apologetic. Even rueful.

He closed his eyes and sighed again. "Believe me, Cait, I don't make a habit of rushing women like that. Never have, as a matter of fact."

Cait's heart sank. He not only looked sorry, he sounded sorry. Once again he'd come up with what she least expected from him. A tactful reply. A sensitive smile. His battered heap of a van. And now, very evident regret at having strayed too far too fast.

She cleared her throat. "Inviting it was out of character for me, too."

"Let's eat, then," he replied, managing a weak grin. "I'm starved."

"Adam—" Cait began, but he was out of the van before she could say she'd had a change of heart about eating at the hotel. Then he was helping her out, and somehow she couldn't say it.

She couldn't say anything coherent for some time after she took the hand he offered and slid down from her seat.

Perhaps it was best she'd brought him here, she told herself as she led him across the beige-toned hotel lobby. Getting involved with this compelling man, wrong as he was for her and she for him, would only end in disaster.

After dinner at Euphoria Adam's misdirected ardor would be certain to cool. As for her own growing desire to know more of him, dinner at Euphoria would be argument enough against such madness. All in all, perhaps it was best.

The plump hostess greeted her like an old friend. "Cait! I saw you on the tube this morning. You were great."

"Thanks, Emily." Cait peered beyond her into the café. Softly lit and decorated like a French bistro, Euphoria was packed as always. Despite her concerted effort against it, Cait felt her heart lighten. Maybe Emily wouldn't be able to seat them. Maybe discouraging Adam with dinner here wouldn't even be a possibility. Maybe there was a gentler way to deflect his unwelcome attentions.

"Table for one, as usual?" Emily asked.

Cait winced inside. Much as she wanted to discourage Adam, she wasn't quite that anxious for him to know she usually dined here dateless.

To her further chagrin, Adam spoke up behind her. "We're two tonight, Emily. And we'll need a quiet table, please."

Emily's eyes shifted from Cait to Adam and widened. Her jaw dropped. "Oh, my! You're him... you're—"

"Yes, I am," Adam admitted, "which is why we need something out of the way."

"Oh, my— I mean, certainly, Mr. Webster."

Cait blinked at the familiar hostess as if at a stranger. Well into her sixties and heretofore unflappable, Emily might have been a teenager meeting a rock star in the flesh.

Flushing one flustered shade of pink after another, she showed them to a table in a side alcove. All around, Cait noticed, the heads of other diners turned to follow their progress. The buzz of voices in the room rose.

"Adam Webster..." she heard from the left.

"... wrote those running books..." she heard from the right.

She glanced back over her shoulder at Adam. His expression was blank, impassive. In that moment the fact hit her with full force for the first time since she'd crossed swords with him in the studio: Adam was famous, superstar-famous, name-famous, face-famous. And she, Cait Rafferty, had walked right into Euphoria with him without thinking.

Just as she'd begun praying for a hole in the floor to swallow her, she heard one loud whisper rise above the rest. "... that TV cook, Cait..."

It was too much all at once. Head whirling, she tripped on her own feet. Adam's hand closed around her elbow, steadying her, and stayed there until they reached the table.

"Congratulations," he said after they were seated and Emily had left them with their menus. "One day on *Northwest Live* and you're a celebrity."

"Me? What about you? Most of the fuss was over you," Cait objected, still stunned at being recognized so quickly.

Adam shook his head. "Credit where credit's due, Cait. I heard your name float by more than once."

"And your own ten times over," she demurred, loath to dwell on her sudden, unanticipated loss of comfortable anonymity.

"Much ado about nothing," Adam muttered, and Cait watched, astonished, as a hint of crimson tinged the tanned planes of his cheekbones.

Oh, Lord, she thought, forgetting about herself for the moment. Was he shy, too? Tactful, sensitive, unpretentious and shy? He had to be. No man could summon up a blush like that at will.

Her heart sinking again, she asked, "You don't like being recognized?"

"I did at first," he said with a pained smile, "but it gets old fast, believe me."

Cait twisted her napkin in her lap. Oh, why had she brought him here? Where was her customary caution? Underneath it all, he was not the man she had thought him at first. The man he was turning out to be was . . . well, charming and nice enough that he didn't deserve what was in store for him at Euphoria.

She glanced at his menu, still unopened, and seized on a temporary solution. She had to delay his opening it until she decided what to do. Barrage him with questions, engage him in scintillating conversation, anything to keep him from opening up that menu and discovering her little scheme.

"So fame exacts a steep price, does it?" she asked hastily.

He nodded. "More than I'm prepared to pay. I've found it's best to keep as low a profile as possible. That's why I moved here from New York."

"And keeping things low-key is why you drive that beat-up old van instead of a Mercedes?"

"Yes," he admitted with a chuckle. "But it's practical, too. Holds running gear for marathons and bicycles for triathlons."

With every word Cait's heart sank a notch lower. With every word he was turning out to be nicer and nicer—except for the bicycles and triathlons. But that was minor. In another minute he'd be a dead ringer for Clark Kent minus the glasses or the nerd factor. Drat!

"You mean you don't have one single status symbol cluttering up your driveway?" she pursued.

"Not even a BMW." He said it with a sheepish smile. "Disappointed?"

Devastated was more like it, Cait thought as she shook her head and searched her brain for further diversionary tactics. "Er, no suits by Armani, or shoes by Gucci, even?"

"Designer suits, yes. But I can't really say about the shoes." He stretched a long leg out from under the table and scrutinized the plain Loafer he wore, adding, "I don't know where she got these."

To cover up the sudden, unwarranted twinge she felt at that "she," Cait quipped, "Well, I wouldn't know a Gucci if it stepped on me, to tell you the truth."

"Neither would my mother," Adam replied. "She just buys whatever she thinks I need when it's on sale and sends it to me like she did the shoes. Her way of mothering me long-distance, which I happen to love."

Cait's twinge vanished, but her qualms multiplied tenfold. The last thing she needed was a doting mother to add to his growing list of assets. Worse, his mother sounded like hers. A real jewel of a mom.

"She still lives in upstate New York," he went on. "That's where I'm from."

"And the rest of your family?" Cait asked, moved by the note of affection in his voice to draw him out on a subject close to her heart, too.

"I'm an only child." He cleared his throat. "My father died when I was fifteen."

Cait cleared the sudden lump in her own throat. "I'm sorry."

"Me, too. He was a great guy."

They were silent for a moment, and then Adam asked, "What about you, Cait? Are you a transplant, too?"

"No. Seattle born and bred, that's me. My parents live a few miles north in Edmonds. I'm an only child, too."

He smiled, the line of his lips soft and vulnerable. "They must have been glued to the TV set this morning."

She shook her head. "They're in Hawaii for their thirtieth anniversary. Not that they didn't want to cancel the whole trip when they heard I'd be cooking on the show. I had a heck of a time convincing them to go."

"How do you come to be cooking for the show?"

"By way of a newspaper, believe it or not." Cait settled back in her chair, glad for any excuse to retain his undivided attention for a few minutes longer. "After majoring in journalism at the University of Washington, I landed a job as a rookie reporter at the *Seattle Examiner*. When the food section editor had a baby and decided to stay home and play mom forevermore, her assistant moved up to the position and I pinch-hit as assistant. It was catching, though, and *she* ended up jumping ship nine months later for the same reason."

"*You* didn't catch it, though, and ended up being editor, right?"

"Right. Probably because I wasn't married or pushing forty and watching my biological clock tick away."

Adam pursed his lips in a slight reproach. "Talent didn't have a thing to do with it, I suppose."

"If it did, mine was very raw. But I did my best, and it seemed to be enough."

"Why aren't you still there, editing away?"

"My dad would say because I stopped being 'Cautious Cait' for once in my life. Mom would disagree and say I went temporarily insane. Whatever, I quit after a couple of years to teach cooking classes and do that radio spot Shirley referred to this morning on the show. One thing led to another, and I was writing a book on the side. Then Dory took one of my cooking classes and 'discovered' me for her new show."

"You can't be the complete soul of caution and risk live TV at the same time. Risk must win out over the other more often than your father's nickname might suggest."

"I'm getting better at it, I guess."

Just then their waiter approached. "Cocktails for either of you?"

"A glass of champagne for me," Cait said.

"Just water for me," said Adam.

"Perrier or Evian, sir?"

"Neither. Regular is fine."

"Yes, Mr. Webster." The young man bowed and hurried off.

"That's a pretty impressive résumé," Adam said as he picked up his menu and sent Cait's brain scrambling again for a question—any question—that might delay his opening it.

"Uh, does everyone everywhere always recognize you right off the bat like that waiter?"

He laid the menu back down. "Everyone but a certain cook I know." He grinned. "First time I've ever been mistaken for a studio technician."

"First time *I've* ever lost a sure bet to the mystery guest on a morning talk show," she returned, grinning a little herself.

He sat back and fixed her with a steady gaze. "Speaking of bets, how would you like to win the spoils back?"

Cait drew in a breath. It was the last thing she'd expected him to say. Beneath the table she felt his knee press against hers. Above it his eyes invited her answer. In her head the question echoed.

Would she like to win the spoils back from the victor? Was a Hershey bar chocolate? Was Willie Wonka her all-time hero? Or was this the sort of proposition a smart cookie turned down on the spot if she knew what was good for her?

"Just what did you have in mind?" she asked warily.

"How about an even exchange, Webster-style?"

"What's that supposed to mean?"

"Well, you lost our little bet this morning your way. Now I'm giving you the opportunity to regain your loss—my way."

Cait's eyes narrowed. "If I remember correctly, you have an annoying habit of hedging your bets to your own advantage."

"What's *that* supposed to mean?"

"Just that you didn't win truly fair and square today, and you know it," she said in no uncertain terms.

His knee went stiff against hers as his eyebrows drew together in a dark frown. "I didn't? As I recall, I forced that junk-food monstrosity of yours down without a word of complaint. Fair's fair, Cait."

"Junk-food monstrosity!" She jerked her knee away from further contact with his. "Why, you . . . you—"

"Try 'health-nut jock.'"

Cait gritted her teeth. "You started it all with that 'artery clogger' business, Adam."

"It did the trick, didn't it? It got you riled up enough to forget you were frozen stock-still with stage fright, didn't it?"

Her hand flew to her suddenly astonished mouth. "You knew?"

He nodded and his eyes thawed somewhat. "I'd been watching you for some time from behind the lights."

Cait could only stare at him.

"At first it was because lavender is my favorite color on a woman," he continued after a moment. "You caught my eye right away. Once I started looking, I couldn't stop . . ."

His voice trailed off, and Cait watched his gaze drop from her face to linger at the V neckline of the lavender silk dress she still wore. She felt it as an almost palpable touch, felt her flesh gather and bud where he had touched her during the kiss in the van.

With another man she might have remained unruffled and discouraged his gaze with a disdainful glance. The few men she'd dated in the years since Doug, however, had never looked at her quite like this. Nor had any of those few stirred as many elemental reactions in her as Adam seemed able to stir at every turn.

With so little experience at her disposal, the best she could do was to lift a defiant chin to meet his gaze and silently curse the discomfiting flush rising to stain her cheeks.

It did her precious little good. When the waiter returned with their drinks a few seconds later, Cait was beginning to squirm under Adam's enigmatic scrutiny. Heaving an inner sigh of sheer relief at the interruption, she took a long swallow of champagne and vowed never to fall into that particular trap again. By the time the waiter left, she was composed enough to raise her glass to Adam's in a gesture of truce.

"Cheers," she offered. "Now, where were we before we started to scratch and bite?"

He tipped his glass to hers. "The subject was even exchanges, Webster-style."

"And stage fright," she added. "How do you know so much about that dread disease, by the way?"

He shrugged. "Some other time. I'd rather discuss the bike ride right now."

Cait wrinkled her nose in distaste. "Bike ride? What bike ride?"

"The one we're going on together, come Saturday," he said with the greatest of ease.

She blinked at him over the rim of her glass. "We?" she sputtered.

He nodded. "That's the deal. You come with me to Lopez Island for a bicycle ride and I return the Cuisinart intact. Even exchange."

"I can't. I don't have a bike."

"I have four. Take your pick."

"Uh-uh. I wouldn't be able to sit down for a week."

He lifted a challenging eyebrow. "It's your Cuisinart, Cait—or could be."

Cait thought about the offshore island, Lopez, accessible only by Washington State Ferry. She'd never been there but recalled reading that it was flat, rural and sparsely populated. Her mind flicked from that to the Cuisinart, all two hundred and fifty dollars worth of it, including attachments. With her bank account in its current dire straits, it would be months before she could replace what she had lost to Adam.

At least the island was flat, she reasoned. But flat or not, she knew a bike ride on it would be hell on wheels for Caitlin Mary Rafferty.

"Okay," she said quickly before her tender tush could vote against it. "I'll do it on one condition."

Adam leaned forward. "Name it."

"Promise you'll clean your plate tonight as proof I haven't steered you wrong where hotel food is concerned."

He beamed and picked up his menu. "That, lady, will be a piece of cake. You've got yourself a deal."

Truer words, Cait thought smugly, he'd never spoken. She sat back with her own bill of fare and congratulated herself for thinking of Euphoria. Faced now with an entire Saturday of unmitigated torture, Webster-style, she couldn't wait for him to open his menu and find her out.

From beneath her lashes she watched him inspect the list of entrées and side dishes. Down one side his eyes scanned and then up the other. Under the table his knee collided with hers as he sat up very straight.

"What the hell?" he muttered.

Cait looked up, wide-eyed with feigned innocence. "Something wrong?"

"This is all they serve here?" he demanded in utter disbelief. "Just . . . just . . ."

Cait broke into a slow, smug smile and nodded. "Just desserts. Welcome to dinner Rafferty-style, Mr. Webster."

4

"YOU'RE IN FOR ONE HELL of a bike ride on Saturday, believe me," Adam growled as he and Cait returned to her apartment from the restaurant.

"You can't say you didn't ask for it, Adam," she growled back.

"I asked you out to dinner, Cait, not dessert."

"A little dinner of amaretto cheesecake and chocolate baked alaska every now and then never did anyone any harm."

"Or any good, either."

"It was delicious."

"It wasn't nutritious."

"What difference does that make?"

"There's a wise old saying that goes, 'You are what you eat.'"

"And another wise one that goes, 'What you see is what you get,' Adam."

"Is that a promise or a threat?"

Cait clamped her mouth shut. An all-time awful night. They'd crossed swords like this from the moment he'd opened his menu and lived to regret it.

She unlocked the door, stepped inside and held out a rigid hand. "Thank you for dinner, Adam, and good night."

He ignored her icy handshake, stepped inside with her and shut the door. "Aren't you forgetting something?"

Cait tensed. Was that an aggressive gleam she saw in his eyes? She hadn't expected this. He hadn't seemed the type to press for more of a good-night than she was prepared to supply. Not after that dinner.

A cold lump of apprehension formed in her throat. Had the verbal sparring done it? She knew that exchanging barbed words had an aphrodisiac effort on some men. It had never occurred to her he might be one of them, though. Oh, Lord. If he was, she had to act fast.

As deliberately as she could, she opened the door and repeated, "Good night, Adam."

He pushed it shut. "You owe me, Cait. I've swallowed more killer sugar and cholesterol today than I've had in months. What's one paltry Cuisinart compared to that?"

"Oh." Relief flooded her. "Oh, I forgot about that."

He lifted a dubious eyebrow. "Very convenient. Just slipped your mind. The big loser of the bet forgets she owes the victor the spoils."

"I did." She gritted her teeth. Back to slice and dice again. "I'll get it for you. Have a seat."

Truffles chose that moment to leap off the couch with an ecstatic feline trill. Cait rolled her eyes as the cat she'd always considered woman's best friend turned traitor for the second time that night and headed straight for Adam.

"Thanks for the offer," said Adam, "but I'm tired of sitting. C'mon, cat."

"Her name isn't 'Cat.'"

He followed Cait into the tiny kitchen and leaned against the counter. Purring like a minimotor, tail held high, woman's worst friend wound a sinuous pattern between and around Adam's long, denim-clad legs.

Cait clenched her jaw and pulled the Cuisinart's plug out of the outlet. The man had nerve following her every move with his grim green gaze—his own special way of rubbing her nose in his victory.

She sponge-rinsed the plastic processing bowl clean and wiped the remains of cookie dough from the machine. If only that rigid smirk on his lips could be wiped off as easily. If only her kitchen weren't so small he almost breathed fire down her neck.

Cait wound the cord around the base of the Cuisinart. Four days without it would be as much fun as dining at Euphoria with Adam Webster. Or as much fun as watching her traitor cat stretch up the length of Adam's leg on the very tippy-toes of her hind feet, as she was doing now, to beg for his attention.

"Down, Truffles," Cait reprimanded sharply.

"Ruffles?" Adam reached down and caressed the adoring little head. "Who'd cook up a name like Ruffles for a brown cat?"

Cait pursed her lips, certain he'd heard right the first time. "The name is Truffles. With a T. As in the ultimate chocolate dessert."

"Oh. Now I get it—sort of."

"You'd comprehend even better if you'd eaten one—or several—which clearly you haven't."

He shrugged. "Can't deny it."

She shrugged. "Pity."

"I'll try not to lose any sleep over it," he said. "Tell me, is Truffles with a T always this affectionate? Or is it just me?"

"She's undoubtedly mistaken you for someone else." Cait gave him a brittle smile and shoved the cleaned appliance into his hands. "There. Good night again and thank you again for the scrumptious dinner."

He lifted a sardonic eyebrow. "I wish I could say it was my pleasure. Where are the attachments for this thing, by the way? Or are you conveniently forgetting them, too?"

"Coming right up," Cait muttered and yanked open a drawer. "Two slicing disks, two shredders, two chopping blades and one wire whisk. Take your pick."

"One of each, thanks. And something to cart it all home in, if you don't mind."

She pulled a big paper grocery sack out of an overstuffed cupboard and slapped it onto the kitchen countertop. "Will this do?"

"Guess it'll have to."

"Good. We're even."

Adam stowed everything into the bag and turned to face her. "Not quite."

"Oh?" Cait inquired. "And what am I forgetting now?"

"How to thank a man properly for dinner."

She retreated a half step. "I thanked you."

"Not with a proper good-night kiss, you didn't. Something to remind us both that I'm a man and you're a woman and what's going on between us doesn't have a thing to do with amaretto cheesecake for dinner."

"There's nothing going on between us."

"Try again. It started with the apron, remember?" He leaned toward her. "And then in the van you kissed me like you'd never get enough."

"So? Who said you had to take it personally?"

"The way you reacted, how could I take it otherwise?"

"No one was holding a gun to your head." Cait retreated another step and backed up against the refrigerator. "Besides, I'm just as entitled to a lapse or two as you are."

"Well, why not entitle yourself to a third one?" Adam closed in and planted both hands flat above her shoulders on the refrigerator door.

Cait lifted her chin. "For two very good reasons, Adam. You're into nutritious and I'm into delicious, and never the twain shall meet. Remember?"

"The way they didn't meet before dinner? Remember?" His voice was gruff, but his hands slipped to her shoulders, gentle and warm.

"Will you please stop harping on that? I didn't wear that apron intentionally, and what happened before dinner was just one of those—"

"Just *two* of those things," he corrected. "Something pretty amazing happened both times. We took to each other like . . . like frosting to cake."

"Neither of which you quite relished tonight at dinner, Adam."

"Maybe not. But there's something right here I could more than relish tonight. Something sweeter . . . more tempting . . . more euphoric than anything they serve up at Euphoria . . ."

Cait kept her gaze pinned firmly on the ribbed neck of his black wool sweater. Meeting his eyes would be too great a risk. Moving even an inch would be too much to dare. A slight step forward and her breasts would press softly into his chest. A tilt of her head and her lips would be fair game for his. Angry though she was, any closer and a third lapse would be a done thing.

Adam's hands slid from her shoulders to her upper arms. "Admit it, Cait." His fingers pressed into her flesh. "Nothing Euphoria dishes up can hold a candle to what happened when we first got a taste of each other."

Cait's head snapped up. "Oh, it can't, can it? I'm the dessert expert here, and I'll have you know that chocolate baked alaska is sweeter by far than . . . than—"

"Cait, something's happening on a deeper level than dessert here, and we both know it."

She lifted her chin and met the green fire in his gaze with the coolest gray stare she could manage. "Whatever it is, it's not based on any great community of interest."

He shrugged. "I'm an only child. You're an only child. That's a start."

"Yes, I'm an only child who happens to adore chocolates you've never heard of before."

"I've managed to survive that major defect without a truckload of regrets."

"Furthermore, I don't have one leg warmer or leotard to my name," Cait persisted.

"My wardrobe's short on both counts, too."

"Adam, the last time I went for the burn was with those chocolate chunk cookies."

"Include me in. I'm still suffering from smoke inhalation."

"Last, but never least, I do not run."

"You're running now, Cait, from yourself and me."

"Oh, you bet I am. I'm moving real fast, backed up against my own refrigerator by a sore loser."

Adam slid his right hand down her arm to her left wrist and circled it in a warm clasp. "I'm the expert on running here, and your pulse is doing a three-minute mile."

"If so, I'm not working up a big sweat over it."

"Oh. Well, maybe you've just mistaken me for someone else. Like Truffles did."

Cait compressed her lips into a stubborn line, pushed him out of her way and headed for the front door.

"Cait—"

"Don't forget the spoils, victor."

He swiped the grocery bag up in one arm. "I'm not forgetting anything, dammit. Not the smallest detail."

"You're forgetting to leave."

"Don't bother to show me out."

"It's my *pleasure* to show you out."

"With pleasures like that, who needs Euphoria?"

"Do I still have to see you on Saturday, as agreed during dinner?" she inquired icily as she swept the front door open for him.

Eyes ablaze, he strode to it, caught her around the waist with his free arm and jerked her against him. Before she could close her startled mouth, he kissed it, hot and hard and quick.

"You'll see me before then," he muttered when he let her go a breathless instant later. Then he was out the door, slamming it closed behind him.

Several moments passed before Cait was able to shoot the dead bolt into place and lean, stunned, against the door for support. Her body shook all over with a mixture of rage and frustration—and more. In the distant reaches of her mind she knew it was a raw, aching desire evoked by the heat of Adam's mouth on hers.

She drew a long, tremulous breath and touched her fingers to her lips. They felt seared, swollen—and still startled. She pressed her burning cheek against the cool door panel, wishing she knew what to do about a kiss like that. Or about a man who could deliver it with as much conviction as Adam Webster just had.

Her hands curled into helpless fists. She told herself he was infuriating. More than anything else, she should be infuriated by him. That was what she should be concentrating on right now. Not the imprint of his lips like a live exclamation point on hers.

But even after she showered and slid into bed an hour later, the electric, erotic sensation persisted. It made her wonder what other electric, erotic sensations a man like Adam Webster might evoke in her, given the opportunity he'd been denied tonight.

WAKING THE NEXT MORNING was as simple as getting to sleep had been. Drugged with dreams of Adam, Cait fumbled for the bedside phone when it sounded a shrill reveille.

"Sweetcakes, it's me."

"Dory, wha—?" Cait mumbled. She opened one groggy eye in a narrow slit and examined the alarm clock. Six a.m.

"Sorry to rouse the dead like this, but today's script's been changed. What do you know about vegetables, sweets?"

Cait flopped over on her back and groaned. "What-ables?"

"Veggies, girl, veggies."

"Mmmph . . . give me a sec."

"Sure, sure."

Cait felt for the cigarettes and lighter she kept by the phone. Just one smoke a day, first thing in the morning, couldn't be beat for getting the juices flowing, she found. She lit up, inhaled deeply and forced her eyes open.

"Okay, back to the beginning. Vegetables, right?"

"Right. We're rewriting the script, and you'll need a wok."

Cait grimaced and inhaled a second puff. "Walk? How far?"

"No, no. Wok. As in big, round frying pan."

"Oh." The fog in Cait's head thinned. "For what?"

"A vegetable stir fry. And you'll need oil and ginger and garlic and soy sauce, too. Right away."

"Now?"

"Now! As soon as you can get here. We go on at 10:00 a.m., remember?"

Cait sat bolt upright and choked out a mouthful of smoke. "Hey, wait. This is Tuesday. I'm off Tuesdays and Thursdays."

Dory let out a loud sigh. "Caitie, wake up. We're rewriting *today's* script, and you're in it. The same goes for every day this week, and you get paid extra to do it, so get here on the double. You can handle a stir fry as well as a torte, can't you?"

"Paid extra!" Cait threw back the covers and swung her legs over the edge of the bed. "I can handle anything from asparagus to zucchini and back again for more money. But why the sudden switch?"

"If you'd stay home once in a while, you'd already know. I rang you all day yesterday and half the night."

"I had classes, remember? And I was...out last night."

"With a man, I hope?"

"Er, sort of."

"Who?"

"No one you—"

"Who?"

Cait sighed. Petite as she was, Dory had all the grit and tenacity of a pit bull. The same could be said for her matchmaking efforts. The last daughter in a family of eight, Dory had an endless supply of nephews she kept inviting to rehearsals in hopes Cait might fall madly in love with one or more of them. Cait hadn't, but hope sprang eternal in Dory's feisty, undaunted breast.

"Who?" Dory persisted.

"Adam." It was no use. "Adam Webster."

"*What?* And he didn't tell you what was happening with the show?"

"No. What does he have to do with anything?"

"Everything, girl. That's why we're rewriting like mad. He volunteered to headline the lead segment of the show every day this week."

"He what? When?"

"Yesterday. After you scraped up your torte crumbs and left, he jogged right up to me and offered to get the show off to a flying start by appearing every day. I came up with the brainstorm of you stirring up something healthy with him, and he said it was a crackerjack idea.

What were you two *doing* last night that he didn't mention it?"

Cait shook her head and sighed. "Cutting each other up, mostly."

"Oh, Caitie, don't give me heart failure. You two have *got* to get along. Think of the ratings he'll pull in."

"I'm thinking, I'm thinking."

"Hon, I've got to dash. Get down here pronto, okay? Bye."

Cait dropped the receiver into the cradle and stared at it. So that was what Adam meant with his cryptic parting comment last night. Not only would she see him before Saturday, she'd see him every day this week, too. He'd made sure of it.

It *was* a brainstorm, though, Cait had to admit. Adam Webster and a wokful of stir-fried chlorophyll couldn't miss as an opening segment on the show. Certainly it was an improvement on following the man's jogging pitch with Chocolate Ribbon Torte.

She took another long drag on her cigarette and blew out a fat, lopsided smoke ring. Vegetables. Yech.

AN HOUR AND A HALF LATER Adam sat in a dejected sprawl in Dory's cracker box of an office at the studio. On the wooden arm of his chair his fingers drummed out a restless tattoo. For the fourth time in ten minutes he pulled up the sleeve of his emerald sweat suit and checked his digital watch. "What if something happened to her on the way?"

"She'll be here," Dory assured him from behind her cluttered desk. "Don't forget she has to round up more than a few leafy greens on her way in."

Adam arched an eyebrow. "You're sure she can cook something besides chocolate?"

"Positive. Like I told you yesterday, I discovered Cait when I took one of the classes she teaches downtown. A pasta class. Anyone who can teach *me* to cook fettuccine Alfredo can cook anything."

"She's that good, huh?"

"Better than good, Handsome. Cait Rafferty's a natural."

Adam gave her a glum half smile. "Not when it comes to dinner. I'm still recovering from last night at Europia—or Erronea—whatever it is they call that miserable excuse for a restaurant."

"Aha. Euphoria." Dory nodded sagely. "No wonder you don't sound like the same guy who twisted my arm for her address and phone number yesterday."

"I'm not. My insides will never be the same." Adam rubbed his stomach. Even a predawn seven-mile run hadn't burned off all that sugar and fat. Or the effect of one mostly sleepless night.

For hours he'd lain awake, thinking about Cait and how his double vow to kiss her and laugh with her remained unfulfilled. No way did that last impulsive gesture of his at the door qualify as a kiss. It shouldn't have mattered that much, he told himself. But it did. Cait had begun to matter more than any woman had in a long time.

He couldn't yet put a finger on why, for she was his opposite in so many ways. Still, she intrigued him. She could laugh at herself, for one thing. And thumb her nose at him in a way no woman ever had. Perhaps most important of all, he had to chase her. Dammit, but it felt good to be the pursuer instead of the pursued for a change. He hadn't run into or after any like her, not since he'd acquired fame and fortune.

Even so, he wished he hadn't started spilling his guts to Dory like this. He couldn't help it, though. She had a candid, straightforward, sympathetic manner that inspired immediate trust. And a bred-in-the-bone integrity, too, if his instincts were right. They usually were—except where Cait was concerned.

"If it makes you feel any better," Dory said after a thoughtful pause, "she didn't sound any more chipper than you when I called this morning."

Adam's head snapped up. "She didn't?"

"Uh-uh." Dory hesitated for a moment. "Look, it's none of my business, but why didn't you tell her what was going on when you were out together last night?"

Adam heaved a long sigh. "I kept waiting for that chip on her shoulder to fall off by itself. It didn't."

"Chip?"

"Yeah. The one with my name on it. You wouldn't know how it got there, would you?"

Dory pursed her lips. "It's probably nothing a little patience and persuasion applied by a man of your obvious charms couldn't overcome. And don't ever tell my beloved husband I said that to a handsome upstart twenty years my junior."

"I won't," Adam promised, "and you don't look a day over forty to me, Boss Lady. But what's obvious to you isn't obvious to Cait. She—" He halted at a muffled knock on the office door and leaned forward from his chair to open it.

Cait pushed partway in, a huge bag of groceries in each arm. She wore a pearl-gray raincoat that matched her eyes. A halo of loose auburn curls framed her face, still rosy from the crisp October breeze.

Out of the top of one grocery sack lacy green carrot tops sprouted. Out of the other, celery stalks, parsley, Chinese cabbage and broccoli.

"Oh, it's you—" she said, gasping, and stopped in the doorway. Her glance swooped from Adam to Dory and back again. "Oh—" she repeated in a choked whisper.

Adam rose halfway from his chair. "Here. Let me—"

Behind her desk Dory half rose, too.

Eyes wide, cheeks flaming to deep crimson above the carrot tops, Cait retreated. "L-later," she stammered to Dory, "when you're not busy."

"Sweetcakes, I'm not," Dory protested. "Adam and I were just—"

Cait shook her head and scuttled out backward. The door swung closed. Dory blinked and plopped back down in her chair. After a moment Adam lowered himself slowly into his.

"You were saying?" Dory inquired.

"I forget," he muttered. All he could remember was Cait's face and eyes and mouth. A face that could haunt a man's fitful dreams all night long. Cinnamon-flecked eyes rimmed with russet lashes. A mouth and tongue that could frame a tart reply or ravage a man's self-control with a single searching kiss.

"Your obvious charms, remember?" Dory prompted. "The ones apparent to me and not Cait."

"Oh. Yeah."

"Still think they're not obvious? After the way she bolted out of here headed in three different directions at once? I'd hang right in there if I were you, boy."

Adam sighed. "I don't know, Boss. After last night I don't know what to think."

"Think patience and persuasion. Please. I'm running out of nephews."

"Out of what?"

"Nothing, nothing." Dory stood, her hazel eyes snapping with enthusiasm, and raked a hand through her graying pixie cut. "Up and at 'em, Tall and Dark. We've got a show to get on the road."

OUT IN THE STUDIO Cait tied a cream homespun apron over her pale gray angora sweater dress and turned to her stage-set sink. *Patience*, she told herself as she scrubbed carrots with a stiff brush. *Smooth things over with Adam. Hold your tongue. Think of the ratings he'll pull in.*

Above all, pull yourself together. Wipe the lingering imprint of that last kiss off your lips, get that idiot tongue of yours untied before show time, and never flee the primal, elemental fact of that man's presence again.

For the hundredth time that morning she craved a second cigarette.

She had just finished with the carrots and succeeded at pushing both Adam and the craving out of her mind when two large hands closed around her upper arms from behind.

Cait practically jumped out of her gray suede pumps. Her breath stopped short in her throat as her head snapped around. The vegetable brush clattered from her hand into the metal sink.

"How about if I scrub and rinse and you slice and chop? Orders from headquarters," Adam's husky voice said at her ear.

It took two tries before Cait could clear her throat sufficiently to croak, "Headquarters?"

"Dory. She cracked the whip and ordered me out here to help you." Firmly, but gently, he shifted Cait two steps to his left and took her place at the sink. "Where do I start?"

Cait dried her hands on her apron, caught her breath and bit back the impulsive retort that rushed to her lips. What good would it do to snap, "You tell me, wise guy," when the way her heart was lurching around in her chest, it was sure to come out all garbled and shaky.

Instead she glanced at the heap of unwashed produce on Adam's right and opted for the relative safety of a simple monosyllable. "Sprouts," she said.

"Coming right up." He scooped a pile of fresh bean sprouts into a strainer and swished them under the tap. "After last night," he muttered, "it's the least I can do. Sorry I was such a sorehead."

Cait stood silent for a long moment. She hadn't expected an about-face on his part.

"Well," she finally replied, "I have a sorry of my own to say, I guess. I really shouldn't have taken you to Euphoria." She paused before adding, "I had my reasons, though."

"No doubt. You wouldn't care to share any of them with me, would you?"

"Let's just say I've learned from experience that opposites don't attract, at least not in the long run. I'm not anxious to relearn the lesson, that's all."

"Maybe it's not a matter of relearning anything," he said after a moment. "I mean, no two people have the same perspective on every point." He cleared his throat.

"And we were, ah, in perfect accord on more than one point last night."

Unable to refute the fact, Cait reached for a towel to blot the carrots. She thought of reminding him that the discord between them had outweighed accord two to one, but decided against it. Now that he'd tendered an apology and she'd accepted, he might take it the wrong way. And as Dory had stressed, it was now necessary that Cait and Adam get along.

At the moment there was no difficulty in that. In fact, Cait decided, it wasn't half bad standing there side by side at the sink with him, almost rubbing elbows. There was definitely something in his mere presence that had the power to affect her. She could feel it even now, in the air between them.

So near she could touch him, Adam set the sprouts aside to drain and moved on to rinsing snow peas. Yes, she thought, she and Adam Webster had been in perfect accord at times the night before. She hadn't been able to fool herself into denying that fact. In truth, she had to admit that never had she fit so perfectly into any man's arms as she had into Adam's. Nor had any man's touch, including Doug's, ever had quite the same effect on her.

With covert sidelong glances Cait watched Adam's hands as he worked. They were lightly tanned, with long, lithe fingers. Fingers that had touched her and trailed hot blood in their wake. Even now she had little difficulty in imagining how those hands might savor the curves of her body, his lips and tongue following everywhere he touched, cherishing each feminine secret of her flesh.

A hot, honeyed ache melted lower and lower into her body as she imagined him making love to her, whispering words to her that she craved to hear, loving her in ways she might never have been loved before.

Love! She almost gasped out loud at the thought. Good Lord. She had to cut this train of thought, and fast.

She reached for her knife. Slicing carrots in julienne strips was one sure way of setting her errant eyes and mind back on course. A single slip in concentration and she'd be missing a thumb or two. Reason enough to focus on that instead of on making slow, sweet love with Adam Webster. Fast and furiously, her knife slashed at the first carrot.

"Pretty fancy technique you have there," Adam observed as Cait's expert blade work built up a mountain pile of matchstick strips. "Verrry nice."

"Nothing to it," Cait got out. "Practice makes perfect." She reached for another carrot and tried not to think of how very much more than "verrry nice" more time spent with this compelling man might be.

"Nice dress, too," he added in a husky undertone.

"Why, thank you," she said after a startled instant in which she almost hacked off a finger.

"Nothing to it," he murmured. He turned back to the sink but not before he'd seen the way Cait's lips softened and the way her cheeks turned a flattered and flattering pink.

A surge of renewed anticipation rose in his chest as he stripped the outer leaves off a head of Chinese cabbage. Within seconds he was whistling an upbeat tune under his breath. He thought about adding that he not only liked the dress, but what was in it, too. Then he shelved the thought. Now that he'd apologized and she'd accepted, she might take it the wrong way.

Save it for later, Webster, he told himself. *Like she said, she has her reasons. With experience as her teacher, who says she can't unlearn a lesson learned? Be patient for a change. Dory just might have a point.*

5

TEN PAST TEN on the big studio clock found Cait staring into her heated wok as Adam and Shirley wrapped up the lead segment on Tuesday's show. She closed her eyes, swallowed hard and tried to remember that she'd gotten through Monday's show without fainting dead away on the set.

Today, though, was a different story. Today she had no memorized routine, no recipe timed with precision down to the last second. Today she had to wing it with Adam, which meant improvising on the scanty script Dory and the writers had sketched out for the cooking spot.

"I want you two to lock horns, like Tracy and Hepburn, right off the bat," Dory had told Adam and Cait during their last-minute rehearsal.

Cait had blinked at her. "Tracy and Hepburn? Us?"

"Yep. You'll be a smash together—the Contessa of Chocolate versus the Sultan of Sweat. Keep it sassy, keep it snappy, and don't set foot on common ground together until the end. Even then, make it an armed truce."

Cait's head still whirled with all the hurried instructions and chaotic coaching. She forced her eyes open and gripped the edge of her counter with both hands. Adam was stepping up into the kitchen to join her. His interview segment about the joys of low-fat, high-fiber eating was finished, and Cait hadn't registered one word of it.

"Take it easy," he said as he took his place beside her. "We've got a whole slew of commercials between now and the time we go on."

She nodded and gripped the counter even tighter.

Adam's hand closed around her wrist. "Just hang loose," he murmured. "If you blow a line, ad-lib whatever pops into your head like we did at rehearsal. It worked then and it'll work now."

She squeezed her eyes closed and nodded again.

"Cait, look at me," he commanded in a sudden, hard whisper. "Let go of the counter and open your eyes."

"I c-can't."

"Stop this and look me straight in the eye right now, or I'll—"

"C-can't b-breathe," Cait chattered.

"So help me," he hissed, "you shape up or I'll . . . I'll kiss you the minute we hit the air."

Her eyes flew open and met his. The startled protest she uttered came out in a strangled gasp.

"Forty seconds!" a voice called out.

"I will. And I'll enjoy it." His voice was a low growl, his hand on her wrist a steel band breaking her grip.

Cait stared into the green glitter of his eyes and found her fugitive tongue. "You wouldn't," she replied in a shaky whisper.

"Who's going to stop me?" he inquired belligerently, his face inching closer to hers.

"Me . . ." She shrank back a little.

"Who?" he demanded.

She balled her hand into a fist. "Me," she said in a firmer tone.

"What did you say?"

"Don't," she snapped and wrenched her hand from his grip.

"Thirty seconds!"

"Don't what? Don't kiss you like I did last night?" Adam pursued.

"That was no kiss!"

The harsh, threatening line of his mouth relaxed into a wide, white grin at her words. "You're quite right. I intend to make it up to you later if you'll let me."

Cait glared. "Adam, this is hardly the time or place for a discussion of what did or did not happen last night."

"Well stated," he murmured with a husky chuckle, "and welcome back from stage fright, Cait."

"Twenty seconds!"

Cait stared at him in total consternation for a moment. Then she swayed a little on her feet as embarrassment replaced the panic in her face and thawed the tension from her shoulders. "Oh, God," she whispered as her mind reoriented itself. "I did it again. Just like yesterday."

"Don't sweat it," Adam soothed. "Just plaster that pretty smile of yours on your delectable lips like you did yesterday and we'll both be in business."

"R-right. Like I did yesterday." Cait grimaced, her apprehensive gaze fixed on the camera turned their way.

"You call that a smile?" he muttered back.

The countdown started. "Ten. Nine. Eight."

"Okay. I'm smiling."

"Atta girl. That's more like it."

"Good," she sighed, "and . . . thanks, Adam."

"My pleasure." Curving an arm around her shoulders and pulling her to his side, he straightened and faced Camera Two with her.

Cait drew in a fortifying breath and held the camera-ready smile. In her stomach, butterflies still dipped and swooped but more from Adam's touch now than from stage fright. How strong his arm was, curved around her shoulders, how solid his lean thigh felt pressed to her soft one. How subtly thrilling was the warmth of his hand penetrating the sleeve of her knit dress.

From there, that warm hand slipped down to the middle of her back. An inadvertent image of it cupped to the curve of her breast the night before crossed her mind. Tiny chills chased up and down the back of her neck at the vagrant thought.

"Three. Two. One. Go."

Camera One lit up, aimed at Shirley on the interview set.

"Yesterday," she announced, "Cait Rafferty whipped up a dream of a chocolate torte from her brand-new cookbook. Today, versatile as ever, she's enlisted Adam Webster's help with an easy recipe to boost your fiber intake and elevate your vitamin quotient. What's cookin' over there, you two?"

Adam's hand slid down Cait's spine to her waist and then dropped to his side as Camera Two started rolling.

"Vegetables, from A to Z," Adam replied. "Right, Cait?"

At his side behind her wok Cait held up a fat stalk of asparagus in one hand, a long green zucchini in the other. She opened her mouth to reply, but nothing came out.

"Right, Cait?" Adam prompted again as he slid the heel of his running shoe onto the toe of Cait's suede pump and stepped down hard.

"Ouch! I mean, uh, right, Adam. From asparagus to zucchini, these are the little monsters we're talking about, folks. Today's recipe—"

"Wait just a minute," Adam cut in as they'd rehearsed earlier. "*Monsters?*"

"Take a close look, Adam," Cait invited, striving for just the right degree of sass in her tone. "When did you last stroll through the supermarket vegetable aisle for fun?"

"Yesterday," he retorted. "But I do remember a time when I thought of them as monsters, too. Since then I've learned they're quite tame, even friendly."

"How so?" Cait inquired with raised brows.

"Well, unless you've been living in a nutritional vacuum, you know they're packed with vitamins and minerals and prescribed by mothers and dentists everywhere."

"Which only makes all of us nutritional nitwits turn tail and run at the sight of a parsnip or rutabaga," Cait contended with an exaggerated roll of her eyes. Beyond the camera she could see Dory grin and signal enthusiastic approval.

"Come, come, Cait," Adam admonished. "Even a nutritional pinhead has to admit that no one can live on chocolate alone."

"Unfortunate but true," she sighed with a droll smile. "Even *I* have been known to nibble at a lettuce leaf on occasion to balance things out."

"But why settle for just lettuce," he argued, returning the smile, "when you can balance the imbalance and tempt the palate at the same time with today's stir fry?"

"Even the palate of a confirmed chocoholic like me? We'll see about that," Cait said, turning to the camera. "The theory is if I can cook it and like it, friends, you can, too. So let's test it by stir-frying two split cloves of garlic in a dash of sesame oil over high heat. Adam, would you please hand me that minced ginger?"

"Anything to tempt the palate of a confirmed chocoholic like you, Cait."

"I'll try to restrain myself, Adam. Now, folks, add a tablespoon of gingerroot and stir-fry a few seconds more, then toss in a cup of drained canned water chestnuts. Oh, Adam, would you hand me those darling little scallions over there?"

Continuing in the same vein, they traded salt-and-pepper verbal volleys with each other over the sizzling wok right to the end of the segment. As the concluding moments of their time slot crowded in, they taste-tested the finished dish together.

Wielding a pair of chopsticks, Cait plucked an asparagus tip out of the wok and popped it into her mouth. Adam did likewise with a broccoli spear.

"Delicious," she pronounced.

"And nutritious," pronounced Adam.

"At long last," she sighed, "a meeting of the minds."

"I knew you'd rise to the occasion, Cait."

"Adam, would you hand me that big, sharp knife, please?"

"Knife? Aren't we through cutting up in the kitchen?"

"Not quite. There's one last monster to tame here."

"Thank you, Adam Webster and Cait Rafferty," Shirley interceded in a chuckling voice-over. "We'll be back in a moment with a famous astrologer who'll tell what our lucky stars have in store for us. Stay tuned."

Cait watched for the video monitor to switch from a sizzling, steaming close-up of the finished stir fry to a series of commercials. When it did, she slumped against the counter with a long sigh of relief.

"Good gravy, you two were fantastic together," Dory raved, hurrying up to them. "Just keep up that twitty little tug-of-war through the rest of the week and we'll pull in every viewer in the Pacific Northwest. Great going, kids." She rushed off again to shepherd the astrologer onstage.

Adam grinned and picked a crisp water chestnut out of the wok. "She's right," he said to Cait. "We were fantastic, kid."

"Speak for yourself." Cait mopped her perspiring face with the hem of her apron. "I'm still the rank amateur, remember?"

"All you needed was one little prompt. Big deal."

"Thirty seconds!" a voice called out. "Cait and Adam, move offstage, please."

"Sure. Sorry," Adam called back. He picked up the wok by its wooden handles and looked at Cait. "How about breakfast?"

She made a face and rubbed her stomach. "That? On top of butterflies? Ick."

He raised an eyebrow. "It's this or butterflies à la carte."

"Twenty seconds!"

"C'mon, Cait. Let's take two in Dory's office." Adam stepped down from the stage with the wok and headed across the studio.

After a moment's hesitation Cait grabbed her chopsticks and followed. It had to beat sticking around to find out what her lucky stars had in store for tomorrow.

Settled in Dory's office with the wok between him and Cait, Adam reminded himself to take it slow and easy. *Forget the effect that subtle perfume of hers has on you*, he told himself. *Forget about wanting to get closer and closer until you know everything about her. Concentrate on right here and now, and keep it light.*

He was gratified no end when his efforts paid off. After a few wary minutes Cait relaxed enough to nibble at the stir fry. Before long, halfhearted nibbles gave way to bolder bites, then moved on to murmurs of approval that matched Adam's.

When the wok was almost emptied, she propped her chopsticks against it and marveled, "Amazingly good, if I do say so myself. I haven't eaten that much rabbit fodder in years."

"I have," Adam replied, "but it never turns out this good when *I* cook it. You have a real knack, Cait."

"Maybe too much of one."

"How's that?"

She grinned and toyed with a chopstick. "I'll probably break out in long pink ears and a fluffy tail any minute now."

Adam chuckled. "If you do, I'll cut you a deal." His voice dropped to an conspiratorial whisper. "You show me yours, and I'll show you mine."

Adam watched the smile quiver on her lips for a moment and then quicken. The corners of her eyes crinkled. The irrepressible giggle still so vivid in his memory bubbled up in her throat. An instant later she released a peal of lilting laughter that was music to his ears.

He threw back his head and joined in. Dory, he decided, was one smart lady. The moment he'd been craving since the night before had arrived.

Cait's eyes were still shimmering with mirth when Adam flipped the switch on the portable television on Dory's desk. "Let's see how the show's going."

"Mmm," she agreed and focused on the small screen. Several moments later, though, she was still oblivious to what was on it. All she could think about was Adam's husky chuckle, the laughter they had just shared, the intimate warmth she couldn't help feeling in his company.

She slid a covert glance from beneath her lashes at him. He was still smiling slightly, his eyes fixed on the TV screen. Little pulsing waves of liquid heat began a steady lapping throughout her body as memory revived the searing feel of his kiss the night before. And the slow burn his touch ignited whenever and wherever he touched her.

She slid her eyes back to the screen, knowing she shouldn't want more of this warm closeness surrounding herself and Adam. Or more of anything else.

She shivered slightly at the turn her thoughts had taken and redoubled her concentration on the screen.

"More famous people are born under the sign of confident, self-reliant, humanitarian Aquarius than under any other sign of the zodiac," the bejeweled brunette astrologer was telling Shirley. "Many rise from early obscurity to great prominence and fame entirely by accident. While Gemini and Leo mate well with this sign, Libra is the best match of all."

"Libra. That's me," Cait murmured, shaking off her light trance. "September 30."

"So it's wedding bells ahead for all those Aquarians and Libras out there, is it?" Shirley inquired with polished, hostly interest.

The astrologer nodded. "Indeed it is. And a match made in heaven, too."

"Thank you so much for visiting with us today." Shirley shook the woman's hand and turned to the camera. "We'll be back again tomorrow with Adam Webster, Cait Rafferty, and a dream expert who will tell you what your nightmares *really* mean."

Adam turned the set off and rocked back in his chair, thighs spread, hands clasped behind his head. "Do you believe in astrology, Cait?"

"I know my sign. That's about it. I guess it's more curiosity than belief with me." Cait crossed one leg over the other and swung it in a nervous arc. She wished he hadn't lounged back quite like that. Suddenly the office seemed smaller and even warmer than it had the moment before.

He nodded. "Me, too. Not that I'd want to be caught dead at a cocktail party asking someone, 'What's your sign?'"

"I wouldn't, either," Cait replied, shifting in her chair. "But I *do* peek at my horoscope in the newspaper every now and then. Don't you?" She uncrossed her legs and recrossed them in the opposite direction. If only his pose didn't accentuate the masculine planes of his chest beneath the emerald top of his sweat suit. If only the juncture where the inseams of his matching pants met would stop being the focal point it had become. The combination of the two was a more potent reminder of Adam's devastating masculinity than Cait's libidinous senses needed at that moment.

"Peek at my horoscope? Now why would a confident, self-reliant, famous guy like me do a thing like that?" Adam drawled. He straightened a little in his chair and slid his hands deep into his pockets.

The smile on Cait's lips froze. "You aren't— You can't be."

"Can't? Why? What's wrong with being the humble possessor of a humanitarian quality or two?"

"You can't possibly be an Aqua—"

"Believe it or not," he cut in, "I'm all of the above and a Scorpio, too."

"Ah, Scorpio. I might have guessed." Cait offered up a silent prayer of thanks that he wasn't her perfect match and that he had shifted from his unconsciously provocative position. She could breathe again. With less effort.

"You're familiar with the species?" Adam asked.

She nodded. "I was engaged to one a few years ago."

"Not a match made in heaven, I take it."

"We didn't see eye to eye on most things," she said with an only slightly regretful shrug.

"That's what engagements are for, I imagine," he murmured, "though I can't say I know from experience."

Cait tilted her head to one side. "You've never been engaged?"

"No, or married, either."

"Shhh. Don't say that within earshot of Dory," Cait warned in a bantering stage whisper. "She has more than a few nieces she's dying to marry off. Believe me, I know. I've been threatened with all of their bachelor brothers."

"Thanks for the hot tip," Adam said with a chuckle. "I'll corner her the minute she comes in."

Cait gave him a sideways smile of total disbelief at the idea of his cornering Dory or anyone else to arrange a blind date.

"I'm serious," he insisted. "I'm dying to get married and live happily ever after. Awful thing for a man to admit, isn't it?" He heaved a mock hopeless sigh. "Maybe it's the long pink ears and the fluffy tail that's working against me. What do you think?"

Cait pursed her lips in a teasing smile. "Lay off the stir fries for a while and see what happens."

"Can't. I'm hooked."

"Sounds like a personal problem to me."

"You're no help."

Cait shrugged. "That's Dory's department, not mine. Odds are there's one marriageable niece in the bunch with a taste for the bizarre."

"Maybe so." He heaved another woeful sigh. "Then again, maybe it's not the ears *or* the tail. Maybe I'm just a slow starter."

"You weren't last night," Cait tossed back before she could think better of it. When she did, she snapped her mouth shut and made a bad job of not blushing.

There was a momentary pause during which Adam's searching gaze held her discomfited one. "You gave me good reason with that apron. It's not every day I meet a woman I can sweep off her feet at her own request. It does something to a man to be invited like that, Cait," he murmured, "something a little crazy."

"I . . . hadn't meant to . . . I mean, wear it, actually," Cait got out. "I just put it on like I always do."

He dug his hands deeper in his pockets. "I'm glad you did, Cait. Aren't you, too—even a little bit?"

Cait blushed deeper and hotter. With nervous fingers she smoothed a fold of her homespun apron in her lap. "Whatever the case," she murmured in an evasive reply, "it's a good thing I wore *this* one today, I think."

"Yeah," he replied softly after another pregnant pause. "Losing my head over you in private's one thing. Losing it on live TV I can live without. Which reminds me," he added, "*you* have to lose that stage fright of yours sometime between now and tomorrow, lady."

Cait shuddered in midblush and looked up. "Don't remind me. I've never felt so . . . so helpless in my life."

Adam nodded. "I know. Your head swims, your heart races a mile a minute, and you can't see an inch beyond your own nose."

Cait stared at him dumbfounded. "How do you know that?"

His smile broadened and he tapped his chest. "Meet the only man alive who passed out cold, in living color, on *Denver A.M.* a few short years ago."

"You?"

"Me. I was promoting my first book. They had to carry me off the set on a stretcher. I have the videotape to prove it."

"But you don't keel over now when you go on live and in color," Cait protested. "How did you get from there to here?"

"A lucky break. My next live TV stint was the afternoon of the same day. Sir Nigel Scott and I were—"

"The Shakespearean actor?"

Adam nodded. "We were waiting our turns in the studio green room. A few seconds before my camera cue he noticed my gills matched the color of the walls and idly remarked he'd read my book and thought it stank. It took me all of half a second to go from pea-green to seeing red."

"Like me with that artery-clogger comment," Cait replied with a sheepish grin.

"Precisely. Nigel's an old hand at dealing with stage fright. He learned long ago that it's impossible to be hopping mad and scared stiff at the same time. After the show was over, he taught me how to do it for myself."

"How?" Cait sat up straight, all attention.

"Well, first we have to rehearse our lines until you can do them in your sleep."

"What lines? We won't have a script until after noon at the earliest, and I have a croissant class to teach from one o'clock to three o'clock today."

"So drop by my place tonight," Adam said. "We'll rehearse until we get everything just right."

"Your place?" She frowned.

"No buts. My kitchen's three times the size of yours."

"What are we going to cook in it, though? I'm fresh out of healthy recipes, I'm afraid."

Adam leaned forward. "Tell you what. You tend to croissants this afternoon, and I'll come up with tomorrow morning's recipe tonight."

"Okay," she decided after a moment's thought. "You come up with it and I'll cook it. Give me the address, and I'll be there around six."

"And I'll be waiting with the script and everything we need in the kitchen," Adam added.

"And I'll be free of stage fright before the next show, right?" Cait inquired.

"Guaranteed," Adam replied in a husky murmur. "And come before six if you can. The earlier the better."

The better for what? Cait asked herself, feeling distinctly light-headed at the question. The better to progress from rehearsal in the kitchen to who knows what later? Oh, sweet agony to even think it. Alone with Adam and a whole night ahead? Could she resist what might come of it? Did she truly want to?

"I might be able to manage that," she heard herself say as if from far away.

Only then did Adam release the breath he'd been holding and uncross his fingers in his pocket. Later, he decided, he'd confess to rearranging the precise month and date of his birth to suit more immediate purposes than the absolute truth.

Later, after every lingering regret over her star-crossed engagement was erased from her memory. Later, after patient persuasion coaxed her hesitant heart out of hiding and her bountiful body into his bed.

Only then would he tell her his sign was Aquarius with Scorpio rising. What was a minor detail like that with a match made in heaven at stake?

"AH, SEATTLE IN OCTOBER," Cait rhapsodized aloud as she drove north from her place to the address Adam had given her. Was there anything quite so fine as a crisp, clear Tuesday in October?

She rolled down the car window an inch and let the bracing early-evening breeze nip through her auburn curls. Though she could do without the constant drizzle that passed for winter in Seattle, she loved these first days of autumn. The hint of frost in the air. The first fire of the season crackling in her tiny fireplace.

Had it arrived in icy January, the Maui-Wowie postcard waiting in the mail on her return home from the studio might have evoked a yearning for warmer climes. Today it brought forth not even a sigh.

Cait's lips curved in a soft smile as she pictured her willowy mother and portly father lazing the hours away on the beach at Kaanapali. Seven more days and they'd be home, clamoring to see the videotapes of her first week on TV. After all, it wasn't every day that the only daughter of a truck-stop waitress and a long-haul truck driver made good on local TV.

The stage jitters, however, were getting to be an everyday thing. Cait's spirits drooped at the thought. Then she forced her lips back into an upward curve and turned her attention to the scenery. This was no time for worrying. Not when the season's fiery reds and golds were splashed all around in the trees that were surrendering brilliant leaves to the sidewalks below.

Forget the stage jitters, she told herself. *Forget the bank statement and the overdue notice on the rent that arrived in the mail with the postcard. And for just a few seconds since you met him, try not to think about Adam Webster and what a mini-eternity an afternoon away from him could be.*

She drew in a deep lungful of autumn-crisp air and released it in a helpless sigh. Forgetting the first three items was possible. Not thinking about Adam was impossible.

Did he, too, like curling up in front of a cozy fire on nights like this? she wondered. A subtle tingle of sensual warmth pervaded her insides as she steered her white Ford compact onto the street that skirted the west bank of Green Lake.

The natural oval lake nestled in the verdant basin of an urban park just a few miles north of the city center. Cait had at first been surprised that Adam would choose to live in one of the modest neighborhoods that crowded the hills around it.

On further thought, it made sense. Green Lake was practically synonymous with jogging in Seattle. Just as the lake drew a variety of ducks, green and other wild waterfowl, the paved three-mile path circling it drew walkers, roller skaters, bicyclists and runners of every age and description. It was only natural that Adam had settled nearby, she reasoned. Probably in one of those posh town houses tucked away in the upper hills.

Cait turned uphill onto a side street and started scanning addresses. It gave her a start when she came to Adam's and found his house to be a perfectly ordinary gray-shingled Dutch Colonial with a view of the lake over the roofs of much larger homes nearer the water. After detecting no glimmer or glitz in the entire scene, she pulled up behind his weather-beaten van and sat for a moment to gather her conflicting thoughts.

Adam Webster. Millionaire runner and author. The man whose book made a fanatic of Doug. A Chevy van with peeling paint. An unobtrusive home in an unpretentious family neighborhood. An intriguing man whose eyes could mock and tease yet slide away with an elusive shyness at the most unexpected moments.

Having already made several revisions in her initial impression of him, she was now forced to make another. Her instincts about health-nut jocks were proving faulty at best. And her customary sense of caution had gone haywire, if the frisson of excitement she felt about the next few hours meant anything.

She got out of the car and walked to the door. Never before had she felt this unsettled, this disconcerted—or this breathless at the prospect of seeing a man again.

She smoothed the cowl neck of the deep plum sweater she wore over matching wool slacks. After assuring herself that she intended to keep Adam at bay, she had nevertheless bathed and dressed with the greatest of care. A contradiction at every turn.

"Face it, Cait," she muttered to herself. "You could melt like chocolate in the hot sun for him. You're melting already, just thinking about it."

It was . . . well, it was almost like being in love. Except that she wasn't in love with Adam. Infatuated, maybe. In love with him in the space of two days, no.

"Just remember your old proverb, sweetcakes," she cautioned herself as she stepped up to the polished pine door with the brass knocker. "Of fine chocolate and love, the first is sweeter by far."

Both were completely forgotten in the next moment. Dripping wet and practically nude, Adam swung the door open to her on the first knock.

Cait had never openly gaped at a man, but she gaped now. She hadn't expected this. Jeans and a sweater maybe. Or one of those sweat-suit outfits he wore for the show. But not what confronted her now.

"Nice timing," he said. "I just finished my last lap."

"Lap?" she croaked inanely.

He nodded. "I swim laps in the pool out back."

Cait swallowed hard. "In this weather?"

"Sure. It's covered and heated. Beats swimming in the lake any day."

Oh, Lord. She hadn't expected this at all. Not long, lithe thighs and calves streaming puddles of water onto a varnished hardwood floor. Nor droplets glistening like tiny crystals on the brown-black lashes of glimmering green eyes.

Not—oh, please, not dark, water-slicked hair tapering from a tanned expanse of chest to a narrow, pointed line that ran well below an indented navel into the hip-hugging waistband of one very brief pair of black swim trunks.

Cait opened her mouth and closed it again. Who could form whole words when faced with so much of Adam Webster all at once? Not Caitlin Mary Rafferty.

With an immense effort she directed her eyes upward from that strip of black nylon. His chest was safer, far safer territory—except for the . . . the—

Her stare widened into shock at the vertical scar there.

She took a shaken step back.

It was the palest of pink lines, shaded by dark chest hair. A slender seven inches long, it bisected his chest.

6

ADAM'S EYES TURNED solemn and followed Cait's to the scar on his chest.

"Heart. Double bypass," he said.

"Wh-when?"

He reached out and drew her inside. "I'll tell you later. In the meantime, come in and meet Masuo."

"Masu-who?" was Cait's faint inquiry as he led her down a long hall. She barely noticed the contemporary living room on the right or the paneled study on the left. Heart, her numbed mind repeated like a drumbeat. Bypass.

"My neighbor from down the street," Adam explained. He led her to the back of the house into the kitchen.

"Oh, my," Cait breathed, forgetting about hearts for an awed, admiring moment.

It was her dream country kitchen come true. The walls were used brick, the floor Mexican terra-cotta tile, the skylighted ceiling white plaster and exposed cedar beams. Copper pots and utensils hung from a metal rack above a six-burner gas range in an alcove to the side. At the other end of the long room a cozy fire snapped in a stone fireplace faced by a high-backed leather couch.

At the square chopping-block work island in the kitchen area stood a slight, bald Japanese man in loose white karate garb. Laid out in front of him were three whole fish and several cooked shelled shrimp. On a large tray to the side was a colorful assortment of artfully sliced and arranged fresh vegetables.

"Masuo Tanaka, meet Cait Rafferty."

"Hi, Cait," Masuo said with a smile and no trace of the Oriental accent she had mistakenly expected. He held out a hand, and Cait shook it, judging him to be somewhere between fifty and sixty years old.

"Masuo's a retired sushi chef, here to give you a private lesson." Adam pulled a high wooden stool over to the island and motioned Cait onto it. "He got everything ready while I swam. Have a seat and watch a genius at work while I grab a quick shower."

Adam retreated and Masuo smiled across the island at Cait. "Adam tells me your technique with a knife is quite something. Where did you train?"

"I didn't," Cait admitted with a sheepish smile.

Masuo's slanted black eyebrows rose. "You're not professionally trained?"

"No. I'm self-taught, with a big boost from watching all the superstars demonstrating their recipes and special techniques on TV over the years. And a lot of reading. I read cookbooks the way other women read romance novels."

"Excellent." Masuo nodded approvingly. "Our task will be easy tonight, then."

Cait held up a warning hand. "Don't count on it. I don't know the first thing about Japanese cooking."

"You've never made sushi before?"

"Never, ever."

Masuo laughed and picked up a thin-bladed knife. "Don't worry. I'll teach you enough tonight to get you through tomorrow's show."

"Aha." Cait settled onto her stool. "So this is what I'm cooking tomorrow. Adam promised he'd come up with something, but I never expected this." Cait glanced at the fish and tried not to look as dubious about their round, staring eyes as she felt.

Masuo nodded and laughed. "Not much cooking, really. Only the sushi rice and the shrimp is cooked in this recipe. If you watch carefully and learn quickly, you'll end up with a very tasty, healthful recipe tomorrow. First, we fillet the yellowfin tuna, then the salmon. You'll want to do that before show time."

Cait bent forward to watch as the diminutive sushi master went to work with his keen blade. In the back of her mind those two unsettling words still pulsed with a faint but steady beat. Heart. Bypass.

UPSTAIRS IN THE SHOWER Adam lifted his face to the stinging needle spray of hot water. He had suspected all along, of course, that Cait hadn't read *Second Wind*, his book about the operation and his recovery. Still, he hadn't braced himself for the total shock on her face when she saw the scar. Or was it revulsion? What was she thinking? Damn, if only she had read the book.

Simple shock he could handle, but not revulsion. Not from a woman he wanted as much as he wanted Cait. As he thought of her, his loins stirred with a hunger he knew wouldn't be sated until he had tasted far more deeply of her than he had in the past two days.

During that short span he'd spent most of his waking life tantalizing himself with fantasies of making love to her, of her making love to him. It intrigued him no end, that fundamental sensuality residing in her hour-glass curves, her throaty laugh, her consuming passion for the most sensuous of tastes and textures.

She would be sensuous and passionate in bed, too, he was sure of it. In *his* bed. Tonight. Unless she'd been appalled by the scar. Better that she first laid eyes on it at the front door, though, than in the bedroom.

He turned back to face the shower nozzle, gritted his teeth and switched the spray from hot to flesh-numbing cold. One way or other he would have more of Cait Rafferty, know more of her, mean more to her than he did. Cold showers in October were the pits.

Downstairs Masuo cut a four-inch square of pressed, dried seaweed and cupped it in the palm of one hand. "The seaweed is called *nori*," he told Cait. "It's crisp and salty and forms the wrapper for *temaki*, handmade sushi." Onto the *nori* square he spooned a tablespoon of sweet-sour sushi rice and pressed it into an oval shape. "Now we can top the rice with fish or vegetables or both," he explained. Placing a paper-thin slice of raw fish on the rice and topping that with a dot of hot horseradish paste called *wasabi*, he overlapped the *nori* edges to enclose the filling.

"Now the verdict." Masuo handed the little package to Cait and pointed to a small bowl of soy sauce. "Just dip it in the sauce and take a bite."

Cait dipped with concealed misgivings. Twice in the past her newspaper career had brought her face-to-face with sushi. Both times she escaped the taste test by assigning it to an assistant editor. Now she tasted and prayed she wouldn't lose face with Masuo.

"Why, it's delicious," she found herself saying a moment later. She dipped again and took a second bite. No fishy taste or smell, just delicate and subtle flavors blended together with the slight sting of the *wasabi.* "Mmm-mmm. And a cinch to make, too."

Masuo's round face beamed. "Precisely what your fans will say tomorrow. Here, have one California-style." Deft and quick, he shaped a second packet of the same *nori* and rice, a pink crescent of cooked shrimp and a slice of ripe avocado.

"Avocado?" Adam inquired in mock horror from the kitchen doorway. "What would your ancestors say about *that* departure from tradition, I wonder, Tanaka-san?"

He slid onto the stool opposite Cait, stopping her heart for a suspended moment. He wore a white shirt with the sleeves rolled to the elbow, faded jeans and soft leather moccasins. Cait could see from the shadow of dark hair that showed through the thin cotton that he wore no T-shirt underneath. Bare—except for the scar, Cait thought with an inner shiver.

Masuo's lilting laugh set her heart and mind in motion again. "They'd say I could make amends by getting to my six-thirty karate class on time for a change," he told Adam. He turned to Cait. "Think you can make *temaki* sushi for the camera now?"

"My pleasure, Masuo," Cait replied. "Thanks for the lesson."

While Adam showed him to the door, Cait wandered over to the fireplace. What a cozy nook had been formed with the long glove-leather sofa facing it and thick sheepskin rugs underfoot. In truth, it was romantic as well as cozy, but she tried not to think about that. Besides, romance was hardly a fit subject for thought, considering her most recent discovery about Adam.

She held her hands out to the warm glow and tried to connect him with a double bypass. She had read enough about the operation to know it was performed to circumvent blockages in coronary arteries.

She frowned and stared into the fire. Doug had never mentioned anything about the author of *Runner's High* having a bypass. Or had the operation been performed during her post-Doug era? In those awful months after the breakup she had buried the pain in studying for semester finals. Had the item been headline news? Deaf and blind to everything but her own misery, would she even have noticed?

"You can read all about it in my second book," Adam's voice said from behind her in answer to her thoughts. "Or we can talk about it now."

Cait turned around to face him, startled to find that he had returned, quick and quiet, and now stood only inches away. Her gaze collided with his and locked on to it, her first slip on what she now realized could turn into an effortless slide with no built-in stops. His eyes were green depths she'd willingly drown in, his lashes the thickest and darkest she'd ever seen.

"I've never read either of your books. I had no idea," she murmured, suppressing a sudden impulse to smooth his hair, still damp from the shower, back from his forehead.

He shrugged and moved closer, his expression half-wry, half-wary. "I could have mentioned it, I guess, but . . . hell, what does a guy say? 'Hi, I'm Adam Webster, the one with the double-bypass. The one who has to exercise and watch his diet like a hawk unless he wants to end up like his father before him.'"

"Diet?" she repeated in a comprehending gasp. Her eyes widened. "And I took you to Euphoria? And you ate that whole— Oh, Adam, you should have—"

"It wasn't crucial," he cut in. "I can indulge occasionally."

"But if it's really bad for you— If only you'd said something, I—"

"I couldn't. I would have had to explain about my dad, how he died at forty of a massive coronary and how I might have ended up the same way without the operation. Great first-date talk."

Cait saw his eyes darken with remembrance and regret. His mouth pulled down at one corner, a vulnerable pull that tugged at her heart.

"Adam, you still should have told me."

"I wanted you to know me better before I did. You were shocked enough as it was, Cait."

He looked so somber and vulnerable that now Cait did give in to impulse. She touched the fingertips of her right hand to his chest, directly over his heart.

"Yes," she admitted softly, "I was, but—" her fingers registered the quickened beat of his heart as she hesitated and then went on "—now that it's worn off, I'm more surprised than shocked. You look too . . . healthy to have had a heart attack."

"Actually I haven't had one. I just came close with chest pains and shortness of breath. The cardiac stress test my doctor insisted on, not a heart attack, put me on the operating table. I was lucky."

"But . . . you look so healthy."

"I *am* healthy, Cait." He covered her hand with his and pressed it hard against his chest. "Feel that. It beats just like any other. I can match any man my age mile for mile on a run, or lap for lap in a pool."

And match any man climax for climax in bed, too, he wished he could say and then prove it to her right there on the sheepskin rug. The leaping flames could make a glowing halo of her vibrant auburn curls. The firelight would flicker on the lush curves of her body, warming her under his hands as he slid her soft cashmere sweater off.

Through the thin cotton of Adam's shirt Cait felt the rich tracery of chest hair and under it hard muscle. His skin there, she already knew, was burnished to a light tan except for his flat, dark nipples—and the scar.

"You can touch," he assured in a husky whisper. "I won't break."

Adam knew that beneath her palm his heart beat strong and healthy, and faster than normal as its rhythm quickened with her touch. But he could tell by the expression in her eyes that the scar still loomed large in her mind.

He couldn't blame her. He'd been in the same fix himself the day the bandages came off. Only by looking at it long and hard and touching it, getting to know it in real terms, had he been able to accept it as a permanent feature of his anatomy. Like a birthmark or a mole.

Cait, too, would have to do the same if they were to go on from here. If she couldn't, he wanted to know it now and not later when the sting of her rejection would be keener. Very slowly he lifted his hand from hers, unbuttoned his shirt and pulled it open.

Cait's hand fell away to her side. Her gray gaze lowered to his bared chest and then flicked back up to his eyes. "It doesn't hurt?" she asked in a voice that held a trace of a wince.

Adam shook his head. "Not anymore. Not even when I laugh. Go ahead, touch it again." His mouth curved slightly at the memory of the times they had laughed together, and then sobered once more. What was she thinking?

If she recoiled, there would be no recourse, he knew. It was one hard, painful truth of the many he had learned since the operation. Even women who had read *Second Wind* and knew his story could recoil. It was one thing for them to read about it, he discovered, and another for them to deal with it in the flesh. Many proved deathly afraid of waking up the morning after with a corpse. Or, worse, feared he'd expire at the peak of pleasure—his, not theirs. He hadn't felt about any of them, though, as he was coming to feel about Cait.

Cait took a small step back, smashing his hopes for a bottomless moment before stepping forward again. Then, just as deliberately as he had unbuttoned his shirt, she lifted a fingertip to the top of the scar. He kept his eyes on hers as she traced it all the way down and back up again.

"Smooth," she murmured, soft surprise in her voice. "I can hardly feel it, it's so smooth."

Don't move, he told himself. *Let her memorize it, reduce it to normal in her mind by touch and sight. Fine, she's doing fine. Discovering there's nothing to fear.* He hadn't expected, though, that she would spread her fingertips out and brush them lightly over the surrounding area in a soft caress.

Oh, God, he thought, closing his eyes. *Both hands now, yes, and don't move or she'll stop. Don't stop.*

Not moving was torture. Not only did his heart threaten to override his self-control, but lower down he felt the ache and swell of pent-up desire. He clamped his eyes tighter shut and fought the urge. Then he felt her palms flatten against him and slide up to his shoulders.

"Adam?" he heard her whisper.

He drew a deep, steadying breath and opened his eyes. "Yes?" he inquired as he exhaled.

"I'm—" She couldn't believe she was touching him like this, but it felt so good she couldn't stop. She glided her palms back down to his chest and splayed her fingers out on him. "I'm glad you told me like this."

"Me, too. I'm glad you're, uh, taking it like this."

Oh, it was easier by the second to slide her palms up the strong planes and contours to his shoulders. Touching Doug had never felt like this.

"Cait," he almost groaned, "do you know what that's doing to me?"

"Yes. If it's the same thing it's doing to me," she murmured, "yes, I do. It makes me want to—"

"Do it, Cait."

With a long sigh she leaned into him. His body reacted before his head did as he pulled her into his arms and crushed her close. Strung taut as he was by her touch, the exploring trail of her fingers still hot on his skin, he couldn't wait for his brain to catch up. He had to feel her against him or he'd explode.

Cait curled her arms around his waist inside his shirt and pressed her cheek to his chest with a shaky sigh of relief. He wasn't perfect. Oh, sweet heaven, he was as imperfect as she was in her own way. And he felt so warm and good to the touch.

"Cait, Cait," he whispered into the curly tendrils at her ear, "I've been wanting this too long."

Tiny streamers of pleasure rippled through her at every point of contact with his body. All man. So strong. So warm. The penetrating heat from the fireplace interlaced with that pervasive warmth, coupling his manly scent of soap and clean skin with a hint of wood smoke.

"I know. Me, too," she whispered, amazed at blurting out what she hadn't fully admitted even to herself until that moment.

"Kiss me, sweet," he coaxed in a husky whisper. "Kiss me like you did last night."

His arms tightened around her, and she breathed in his clean scent knowing there was no stopping the slide now. Saying what was in her heart had only added to the headlong momentum she knew would not now be easily slowed.

She tipped her head back to look into his eyes. They were a green blaze in the firelight, so close she could barely focus. Only barely could she breathe, too, so tightly was he holding her, so close were his parted lips to hers.

"Kiss me, Cait, for God's sake, before I—"

He broke off as her lips brushed his in an answer she couldn't withhold. Her lashes fluttered, then her eyes closed as she pressed her mouth to his. She felt his hand leave her back and move up through her hair to cup her head.

He has lips like no other was her only thought as they molded to hers, mobile and moist, lined with fire. The way he had of moving her head to his in an erotic, circular motion—she had never felt anything like the fluid, melting ache it evoked in her most secret places. His slim hips pressed into the softness of hers, and she felt the hard swell that proclaimed him man.

Never detaching his lips from hers, he pulled her down with him onto the sofa. Cait sank deep into the plush glove-leather cushions and moaned slightly in her throat when he stretched her out between his long body and the high curved back.

Only when she was fully reclined, her legs and arms entwined with his, did he break the kiss and draw a long, uneven breath that echoed hers.

"You must know by now," he murmured, "how much I want more than just a kiss." He slid his hand around from the back of her head to fit it in the same curve over her breast. "You do, don't you?"

Through her sweater Cait felt the heat of his fingers. "I don't usually move quite this fast, Adam." Even as his name passed her lips, though, her breast swelled into his hand. Beneath it her heart pounded as if she had run up several flights of stairs without stopping.

"What *do* you usually do?"

"I exercise a measure of caution."

"I understand," he soothed. "I'm not the free-and-easy type, either. I didn't risk my heart at Euphoria for a one-night stand."

"Why not?" she felt compelled to ask in a breathy murmur.

"I want more nights than just one for us, Cait. Many more." His palm flattened and began to rotate in slow circles over her budding nipple. "There's no other woman in my life, either, if you're wondering."

Cait sighed and moved her body in response to the stroking. "No other— Adam, that feels so . . ."

He slipped his hand under her sweater. "Anyone in yours I should know about?" he murmured against her lips as his fingers traced the upcurve of one breast to the very tip.

"No."

"Good." He captured her mouth with his again, tempting her with the silky thrust of his tongue until she eagerly surrendered hers to him in return.

His hand continued upward and somehow it seemed the most natural thing in the world to lift her arms and let him slip her sweater over her head.

"Lavender," Adam whispered, tracing the delicate lace pattern of her bra. "You remembered." He unhooked the front catch, and Cait swallowed a gasp of pleasure as her breasts swung full and free to his touch. Her fingers twined in his dark hair as his moving mouth trailed down her throat, hungrily down to where his warm palms cupped and treasured her.

"You're beautiful, Cait," he said, raising himself a little to feast his eyes on her. His thumbs stroked inward as he lifted his heavy-lidded gaze to meet hers.

Cait searched his eyes, wanting to believe him, yet afraid to let herself actually do it.

"You are." The circular stroking of his thumbs neared her taut nipples but stopped just short of its goal when she bit her lip and tucked her chin down. "Hey," he whispered, "what's wrong?"

She forced her eyes back to his. "Do you mean that, Adam?"

"Absolutely." He looked surprised. "Don't I sound like I mean it?"

She bit down harder and then replied, "I don't know how it's supposed to sound."

"You mean...when you were engaged, he never—?"

Cait shuttered her uncertain gaze and shook her head.

"Damned lucky you didn't marry him, then," Adam said in a throaty growl. "If you were mine, I wouldn't let you forget it for a minute. You're lovely."

She lifted her eyes to his again and watched his gaze lower to where his thumbs resumed their inward stroke toward their twin objectives. "Lovely," she heard him repeat as his thumbtips brushed reverently over her swollen nipples.

Her eyelids fell closed. "But I'm not yours, Adam," she said in a last wild stab at reason. "We've known each other all of two days."

He lowered his head and touched his tongue to one pale auburn areola. "We know enough for now," he whispered, his breath hot on her as he circled and probed and curled his even hotter tongue to her.

"Adammmm..."

The long sigh of pleasure that carried his name brought a muffled moan from his throat as he drew her into his mouth and sucked her to a hard throb. What sort of man had she been engaged to, anyway, who hadn't whispered sweet somethings in her ear when he made love to her? A fool, Adam decided, a poor, damned fool.

"I want you so much, sweet," he breathed, thrilling to the feverish play of her fingers in his hair as he gave both nipples equal attention. "You want me, too, don't you?" He lifted himself slightly and brushed the dark down on his chest back and forth over her breasts.

"I . . . yesss . . ." she sighed, seeking out the flat male nipples shadowed in his chest hair and caressing them to stiff pinpoints of sensation. Between her thighs she felt the slide and then the warm press of his hand at the inseam of her wool pants. "Ohhh . . ."

His other hand guided hers down to where he strained hard and thick against the zipper of his jeans.

"Oh, Adam . . ."

"Cait, honey . . ."

"Grrrr!" The low growl came from the kitchen. Cait and Adam froze in midmotion. Another low, menacing growl sounded. A blood-chilling yowl followed it.

Cait gasped and snatched away her hand, raising it to her mouth.

Adam groaned at the loss of her touch and clenched his teeth against a stream of words that begged in swift succession to be sworn aloud.

"Mordecai!" he called out instead. He levered himself up to glower over the high back of the couch in the direction of the kitchen.

Cait grabbed up her sweater and clutched it against her breasts. What manner of man or beast had uttered that bloodcurdling sound? Not man, oh, please, not man.

"Mordecai! Mollie! Mitchell!" Adam bellowed. "The three of you, *out!*"

A chorus of low growls was the only answer. Holding her bra together with shaking fingers, Cait rose to peer over the back of the couch into the kitchen.

Three bristling black shapes were facing one another down, wild-eyed and tense, on top of the island in the kitchen. The biggest and blackest of the three licked his chops between growls. The shrimp, clearly, were history.

Cait stared from them to Adam and then sank back into the cushions with a loud, relieved sigh. "Cats! You have cats!"

"Not for long, if they keep this up," he replied through gritted teeth. "Mor-de-*cai*, do you understand S-P-C-A?"

Cait could tell from the continued glare in Adam's eyes that none of the three considered it the slightest threat. Adam made a frustrated, impotent sound deep in his throat and glanced down at her.

"Don't you dare," he commanded at the amused grin that had begun to play at the corners of her mouth.

She couldn't help it, though. Her shoulders started to shake with silent laughter. Only a man who was a pushover for cats could look so very stern and so very helpless at the same time. It was quite clear who was the paper tiger here. Adam Webster was a slave to his cats.

He broke up, too, when her silent laughter bubbled into sound. Would he ever be able to resist it? he wondered and hoped he'd never see the day. Had he ever known a woman who made him laugh and enjoy it so much? Not that he could remember.

"Cait," he reproved her when he could finally talk again, "that's tomorrow's script they're scarfing up, remember?"

She wiped the tears from the corners of her eyes and pulled in a deep, sobering breath. "I'm sorry, I just—" It was a struggle still to keep a straight face. She breathed deeply again. "I know how it feels. Truffles outnumbers me every time at home. But you—with three—a glutton for it."

"All the more reason for us to put up a united human front," Adam replied.

"Okay." She wriggled up to glare at them as Adam was doing. "How's this? Mean enough?"

"Ferocious," he said dryly. "Is that the best you can do?"

"'Fraid so. Cats melt me."

He sighed and turned to the cats again. "Break it up, you goons," he thundered ominously, "or it's back to the cat-catcher with you."

He might have been singing "Dixie" for all the three in the kitchen appeared to care. He grimaced. "My fault, of course," he muttered. "Forgot to latch the cat door."

Cait nodded. "And forgot to feed them, too, from the look of things."

His eyes roamed down to where she clutched her sweater against her. "I was preoccupied," he said, his voice husky. "Still am, as a matter of fact."

"With tomorrow's script at stake? Don't you think you'd better take care of first things first?" She inclined her head toward the kitchen where a tense, bristling silence now reigned.

"Promise you won't move until I get back." He brushed a light kiss over her lips and heaved himself off the couch. Out of her earshot he muttered a ripe oath. Last night cremated cookies. Tonight caterwauling cats. At this rate he'd be taking cold showers for months. He stalked to the kitchen island and growled out loud.

Mitchell, always the meekest, was the first to knuckle under and leap off the island. Mollie, always the follower, followed. Mordecai, always the ringleader, stubbornly held his ground for a moment. It took a threatening clap of Adam's hands before he dropped his prize catch and sprang to the floor with the others. There the three of them lifted pleading topaz eyes to their master and broke into a chorus of innocent meows.

Cait sank back down onto the couch with an amused smile. Truffles would fit right in with this crowd. Just as she herself had fit perfectly to the shape of Adam's body and hands just moments ago. She pressed her thighs together, still feeling the heat from his palm there.

From the kitchen came the sound of an electric can opener and Adam's voice scolding, "You clowns sure know how to cramp a guy's style." She heard the rough affection in his tone, heard him command softly, "Out to dinner, now, all of you."

There was the sound of a door being opened and closed and then silence but for the snap and hiss of the fire. Cait stared into the dancing flames for a long, measuring moment before she sat up, fastened her bra and slipped her sweater back over her head. Even if she *was* the only woman in Adam's life right now, perhaps it was best the cats had cramped something more substantial than his style. Certainly it wasn't her style to get swept away as she had almost been tonight.

The door opened and shut again, prodding Cait back to the present. She adjusted the cowl neck of her sweater and fluffed her fingers quickly through her mussed curls.

"Cats," Adam muttered when he dropped down beside her and curved an arm around her shoulders. "Now where were we? And why are you wearing that again?"

"Adam—" she placed a hand on his bare chest where his shirt fell open "—I . . . we, you and I—"

He tipped her chin up with a forefinger and touched his lips to hers, stopping the flow of words. "Don't," he pleaded softly. "Don't say you've had time to think and this is all happening too fast."

"But it is. We have a show to do tomorrow and—"

"Listen, I won't lose a shred of respect for you in the morning, if that's worrying you."

Cait wavered for a moment, torn between wanting the touch of his lips to hers again, yet knowing she should take another, saner course of action.

"Adam, two days is no basis for jumping off the deep end," she tried again.

"Two days can be a lifetime, Cait." He stroked the curve of her chin with this thumb. "Listen, one thing a heart patient learns really fast is that time and life are precious. Why waste a second when we feel the way we do?"

"That's just it," she hastened to say, pulling away a little. "Maybe what we feel isn't—I mean, two days isn't long enough for a woman to know a man before she—"

He pressed his thumb into the fullness of her lower lip, gently silencing her. "What about the man?" he inquired. "Is it long enough for him to know her before he lets her make love with him? Or will she think less of him if he does?"

"You know that's not the point," she reproved. "The rules are different for men."

"Then you wouldn't think less of me?"

Cait swallowed hard as his fingers fanned out over her cheek. "It wouldn't be a matter of your 'letting' me do anything, Adam," she protested.

"I'd let you, Cait," he said with a wicked smile.

"Don't tease. I'm serious."

His parted fingers slid, warm and gentle, into her hair. "I like it best when you're not. Where's that sense of humor you've been charming me out of my pants with?"

"*That* wasn't my prime objective."

"Don't look so put out. So I'm a sucker for a woman who can laugh. Would you rather I was just after you for your body?"

"I'm not sure," Cait said, bridling. "What *are* you after me for, anyway?"

"I told you. More than a one-night stand. I'm a one-woman man, Cait. I got the feeling you were a one-man woman."

"I am. More of one than I've acted like tonight. But there's more to a relationship than just that. Two people have to see eye to eye about certain things before they. . . well, you know."

"Get serious?"

"Yes."

"Serious, meaning love or sex?" he inquired, outlining the shape of her ears with a sensuous fingertip.

"Both. I'm just old-fashioned enough to have trouble separating the two." She inclined her head to his touch, unable to conceal her imminent desire to purr like one of his cats under it.

"When was the last time you were serious both ways about someone?" he murmured. His fingers slid through her hair again, raising tiny prickles of exquisite sensation at the nape of her neck. "Or is that getting too personal? If it is—"

"No," she said quickly. "You might as well know, I guess. Doug was the only one."

"Your fiancé?"

"My ex-fiancé." She shivered slightly. "Adam, don't."

"I'm sorry. I didn't mean to pry."

"No, I mean don't touch me like that. Please."

He was silent for a suspended moment before he squeezed his arm around her shoulders and murmured, "Why? Because you like it? Or because you don't?"

Cait took a deep breath and gave him a wavering smile. "Because I, uh, might not respect you in the morning if you keep doing it."

His eyes searched hers for what seemed a small eternity before he released her and started buttoning up his shirt. "Well, we can't have that, can we?" he said thickly. "I'll just have to let the cats back in and wait for the morning you *can* spare me some respect, won't I?"

TWO HOURS LATER, shirt tucked in and script in hand, Adam grinned at Cait across the kitchen island.

"By Jove, I think we've got it."

"Down pat," she agreed, returning his smug grin.

Together they gathered up the sushi ingredients, half of which they'd eaten, and put them away. Cait smiled a little as she worked. Rehearsing, with three cats for an interested, inquisitive audience, had been great fun. And productive, too. If all went as rehearsed, matching wits with Adam again on tomorrow's show promised to be a figurative, if not literal, piece of cake.

"Ready to tackle the stage fright now?" Adam inquired when everything was stored away. He pulled a bottle and two brandy glasses out of a cupboard.

"That's the cure?" Cait said dubiously.

"No, it's Armagnac. Like it?"

"Love it. But is it good for you?"

He nodded as he poured. "Doctor's orders. A glass of wine now and then, a shot of brandy. I just can't overdo." He handed Cait's glass to her and, trailed by Cait and cats, led the way back to the fire.

The M&M&Ms, as Cait had begun to think of them, settled in a purring pile of fur at one end of the couch, and Adam settled at the other. Cait, however, clung to safer territory. Under the pretense of warming her back at the fire, she stood and sipped her drink as Adam settled back and enjoyed his.

"Well?" she prompted after several minutes passed in companionable silence. "What's the first step in Nigel's cure, Doc?"

"After you finish your drink, you lie down and relax." He patted the cushion next to him. "Right here with your head in my lap."

"With my— Wait just a minute here." Cait mentally dug in her heels. "I can't even begin to imagine you with your head in Nigel Scott's lap."

"I'm not asking you to," he soothed. "I sat in a chair. It's more effective if you lie down, though. Trust me. You'll be more comfortable that way."

"Adam—"

"Trust me, Cait." He patted the cushion again. "I'm a man of my word. Just lie down here and relax and stop looking as if I'd just grown fur and fangs."

Cait couldn't help smiling at the ferocious image his innocuous, engaging grin belied. She sipped her brandy through her smile, trying to decide, then drained the glass and set it on the mantel. "Okay," she relented, "but I reserve the right to fight at first bite. Got that?"

"It's engraved on my brain." He drained his glass, too, and set it aside.

A little gingerly, Cait stretched out on the long sofa, the cats at her feet, and pillowed her head in his lap. "Now what?"

"Close your eyes."

She shut them and tried not to think about how close a certain intriguing portion of his anatomy was to her cheek and ear.

"Take a deep breath. In slow and deep—that's it— and out the same way. And another."

Cait breathed as he instructed and began to relax despite her reservations about his methods. His voice was so restful and soothing. Likewise, the contented chorus of purrs at her feet combined with the hiss and occasional snap of the dying fire had a tranquilizing effect.

"Keep going . . . easy in . . . easy out . . ."

She felt the tightness in her neck and shoulders dissolve little by little until her spine seemed to melt under her into the soft leather cushions. "Mmmmm," she breathed, feeling a warm lassitude creep through her limbs, rendering her almost powerless to move.

"That's it. Now visualize the studio and everything in it. Lights, cameras, Dory, the crew. There we are on our set. You have everything you need to make sensational sushi. You know the script inside out and so do I. Breathe normally . . . in . . . out . . . hold the scene like a detailed picture in your mind . . ."

Cait felt the light stroke of Adam's fingers on her forehead now, soothing and smoothing in gentle rhythm with the croon of his voice. She could see everything just as he described it, and as she visualized, her mind seemed to float free on a warm, weightless cloud.

"We're waiting out the countdown now. I'm right there beside you. There's not a thing to worry about, nothing. You know every line you're going to speak, every movement you're going to make, don't you?"

"Yes." Adam heard her sigh. He looked down upon her full, parted lips, her closed eyes framed by long lashes that fanned in delicate, shadowed crescents onto her cheeks. Lovely. He continued to stroke her forehead and temples as his gaze strayed down from her face to rove over the feminine hills and hollows of her supine body. More than lovely.

"Three, two, one, you're on." He closed his own eyes and forced his mind away from temptation and back to the task at hand. "You're delivering your first line. See and hear it in your head. Your voice is just right and so is mine. Our timing is perfect. Just like clockwork we go right up to the end without a hitch, capable and confident. Can you see and hear it?"

"Mmm-hmm . . ." It was the barest of sleepy whispers as she floated higher on her cloud, farther and farther away from reality.

"Now it's over," Adam went on, his eyelids so heavy now he couldn't lift them even to gaze upon Cait's curves. "You succeeded just as you knew you would. You feel wonderful, relaxed, at peace. Keep your eyes closed and hold that feeling . . . you'll feel the same thing tomorrow . . ." His voice trailed away into silence, and his head sank into the back of the sofa.

Several nonsensical dreams later, Cait surfaced slightly from a deep slumber. "Not now, Truffles," she mumbled to the purring weight on her abdomen that kneaded its front paws on her upper chest.

The kneading continued as it usually did when Truffles was intent on displaying her nocturnal affection for her mistress. Still more asleep than awake, Cait did what she always did and lifted the cat off her. Then she rolled onto her side and reached to pull the covers up around her neck so that she could snuggle deeper into her down pillow.

Covers. She groped for them. There weren't any. She groped farther and again encountered nothing.

Pillow. She groped a hand up and felt not a goose-down pillow but a warm something that stirred at her movements and shifted under her head.

No covers. No pillow. She shivered a little at the slight chill in the air as her mind swam up through layers of sleep into dim consciousness.

Her eyes opened, blurred and then focused on faded blue denim. A zipper. A belt buckle and above it white cotton. Good Lord. She uttered a strangled gasp and sat up.

The fireplace was dark, the fire cold ash. The lights in the kitchen behind her still shone, casting long shadows on the walls at her end of the room. She glanced over at a window. It was pitch-black outside and raining pigs and chickens from the sound of it.

Still in an upright position, Adam stirred. "Cait . . ."

"Adam, wake up," Cait urged when his head lolled back again.

"Mmmmm, sweet Cait," he mumbled, reaching out for her with his eyes still closed. "Don't stop, sweet . . ."

Cait pulled back from his sleepy embrace and shook his shoulder. "Wake up, Adam."

"Mmmmm," he sighed when his groggy eyes opened a sliver. "It really is you, isn't it?"

"It's me, all right," she assured him under her breath as she stood and smoothed her rumpled sweater and pants.

He sat forward and rubbed his eyes. "God, what a dream," he marveled in a voice still thick and throaty with sleep. "We were—and you were—fantastic, just fantas—"

"If it's X-rated, you'd better stop right there," she warned, knowing if he went on she'd melt again before she got out the door. "I have to get home and get some sleep."

"Why?" Adam stretched and yawned. "You were doing a pretty good job of sleeping right here with me. Come back here, sweet."

"No. I have to go."

"Why?"

"Because the last thing I'd get is a good night's sleep with you. We have a show to do tomorrow. Be sensible."

"What sense does it make to go out into a downpour when there's a nice warm bed waiting for us upstairs?" He glanced at his wristwatch. "Besides, it's tomorrow now. Three hours into Wednesday."

"Three!? Oh, Lord. Do you have an umbrella I can use between the house and my car?"

"Unfortunately yes." He stood and drew her into his arms. "Promise me one thing before you go, though. Say you'll see me in your dreams."

"I, uh, think it's best if I see you at the studio to-mor—I mean, today."

"What are you doing after the show?"

"Two afternoon classes on chocolate éclairs."

"Think you can fit me in after the éclairs?"

"Only if we stick to rehearsing. I . . . need some time, Adam. To think."

"Okay, you've got it." His arms fell reluctantly away from her. "Go home and catch a few more Zs, but do your visualization first thing after your alarm goes off. And, Cait . . . about that dream we both starred in to-night?"

"Adam, don't start that agai—"

He stopped her with a quick kiss. "It wasn't X-rated. It was beautiful. Like you."

7

"SUCCESS, SUCCESS, how sweet it is. It looks like we're a hit, kids. The letters and postcards and requests for recipes are pouring in." Dory pulled a letter from a heap of fan mail on her desk and read it out loud to Cait and Adam.

"Dear Cait,
I'm like you. I detest vegetables, too, but I made the stir fry, anyway. Would you believe it was good! Better was the Chocolate Ribbon Torte I made for dessert. Now if only you could figure out some way to make sushi out of chocolate instead of raw fish!"

She chuckled and picked out a postcard.

"Dear Adam,
You signed my copy of *Runner's High* yesterday, remember? Are you free Saturday afternoon and evening? If so, I could make it very special for you.
                                  All my love, Samantha"

Dory raised an eyebrow at Adam over the top of the postcard. "Well, Mr. Tall and Dark, are you? Her phone number's right here."

The pang Cait felt at hearing it had not been her first of that week. Samantha was only one of the enthusiastic horde of Adam Webster groupies that had clogged the studio entrances and exits every day. Outfitted in the most stylish of exercise gear, any one of the bunch could have auditioned for the *Twenty-Minute Workout* and been hired on the spot. Cait couldn't help being reminded of the workout clone Doug had married.

Plying Adam with questions, compliments and requests for autographs, they clustered around him whenever he entered or left the studio. Somehow it didn't help that he usually looked as discomfited on those occasions as he did now.

"So sorry, Samantha," Adam said. "I've already made a date for a bike ride on Lopez Island with a cook I know. Right, Cait?"

Cait's twinge of jealousy eased with the reminder. The bike ride. In the breathless whirl of the week she hadn't had much time to think about it. Winging it all the way, she had somehow managed to teach her classes, dream up three more healthy recipes with Adam and rehearse with him every night.

Now, on the Friday afternoon following rehearsal for Monday's chocolate chunk cookies—at long last—she and Adam were winding up the week with an exuberant Dory in her tiny office. The flood of fan mail was overwhelming proof that *Northwest Live* in general, and Cait's cooking spot with Adam in particular, were a hit.

"Well, well. A Lopez bike ride." Dory flipped the postcard back into the mail and glanced from Adam to Cait. She looked ready to comment further when her phone rang. She answered it, listened for a moment and then looked at Adam. "For you. Person-to-person from New York."

His face lit up. "My mom, I'll bet."

"Take it in the office next door," Dory said. She punched the hold button and waved him out. When the door closed behind him, she grinned across the desk at Cait. "Just in case you hadn't noticed, I'll say it again, sweetcakes. That is one special man."

"I've noticed." Cait's smile turned wry. "So have all the Samanthas out there."

"But it's *you* he's taking to Lopez, girl. Perk up. Where are you staying, by the way? McKaye Harbor, the Islander? Wherever it is, cancel the reservations."

"We aren't staying at all. It's just a day trip."

Dory gave her a sly look. "Listen, Gus and I have a getaway beach house on Lopez that's yours for the weekend if you want it."

"Er, I don't think so, Dory."

"It's no big deal. Tons of our friends and family have stayed there. You won't need anything but a tooth-brush. I guarantee it."

"It's not that. It's just that—"

"Good gravy, don't say no until you've at least seen it," Dory cut in. She reached for her handbag and, with all the dramatic flair of a magician plucking a white rabbit out of a top hat, produced a key.

"But, Dory—"

"The freezer's full of goodies. Chocolate Decadence ice cream, even." Dory waved the key tantalizingly at Cait. "Think of it."

Cait threw her a wavering look. "I'm thinking."

"There's a romantic loft bedroom with a view. Think of *that*."

"That's the problem," Cait said with a sigh. "I'm just not the sort of woman who can casually pull that key out after we finish our ride and invite a man to spend the night with me."

Dory pursed her lips. "Things haven't progressed that far yet?"

"Dory, it's only been a week."

"I thought you were rehearsing together every night. Or did I hear wrong?"

"We rehearsed. That's all."

"It must be old age creeping up on me, then." Dory ran a hand through her graying pixie cut and frowned at Cait in exasperation. "I could have sworn you were more interested than *that* in each other. The way he looks at you—the way you look at him. That tone in his voice whenever he says the simplest word to you. Is that it? Am I going blind and deaf, or am I right as rain in Seattle?"

Cait gave in with a smile and a sigh. "Don't worry. You'll need an umbrella before you need bifocals or a hearing aid."

"What's the problem, then?" Dory looked more exasperated than ever.

"Me," Cait admitted. "I'm—"

"Scared," Dory supplied after an appraising moment. "But why? You conquered stage fright in less than a week. What's to be scared of when it comes to that lovely man?"

Cait rolled her eyes. "Maybe you do need bifocals. Why *wouldn't* I be scared? That lovely man and I come from the opposite ends of the earth. He's an exercise guru, for heaven's sake. A jock. To a chocolate freak that's a four-letter word."

"So is cook. But like I said, Cookie, it's you he's spending Saturday with. It's you he's drooling over like a starving man at a feast."

"Why me? Face it, Dory, with all those size seven Samanthas out there at his disposal, what does a man like Adam want with a size fourteen?"

"My dear Cait, you may not be a sylph, but you're no slouch, either. Would I have signed you up for the cooking spot if you didn't look the complete cook and camera-ready, too?"

Cait leaned forward. "That's just it, Dory. I came to terms with what I am a long time ago. But it's not the image books like Adam's push. Why me?"

"Why not you? Isn't the chemistry between you on the show proof enough that opposites attract?" Dory glanced at the stack of fan mail. "Guess how many of them want to know if Cait and Adam are an item."

"You're kidding."

"Not me, kid. That sweet-tart performance you two carried off this week has them asking if you're just like Spence and Kate in those old movies. Read your fan mail, girl. The sizzle shows."

Cait couldn't help squirming a little in her chair. "I haven't had time."

"Read it tonight." Dory grinned a devilish grin. "Unless you have a date with Spence, that is."

"Give me a break, Dory. I've seen Adam four nights running. Like I told him, I need a night to myself."

"Which means five nights running was what *he* had in mind, I take it. Who needs a night to herself with a man like that around?"

"I do. My apartment's a shambles, Truffles thinks she's been orphaned and I need a decent night's sleep if

I'm going to pedal around Lopez tomorrow on a two-wheeled torture machine."

"Okay, sleep. *But—*" she waved the key at Cait again "—take this and warm up those cold feet of yours with Adam tomorrow night."

"Dory—"

"Caitkins, please. At twenty-six you aren't getting any younger. Go for it before you're eligible for Social Security and Medicare."

"I'm hardly a spinster."

"You will be if you don't get off your duff with Adam. Do yourself a big favor."

"Favor?" Adam inquired, walking back in. "Who needs a favor?"

"Me." Dory tossed him the key, and he caught it in a quick reflex motion. "I was just telling Cait how long it's been since Gus and I have been to our weekend beach place on Lopez. If you two wouldn't mind stopping by on your ride to check that everything's ship-shape . . ."

Adam pocketed the key. "Not at all. Be glad to."

"Don't think twice about raiding the freezer or the wine rack or staying the weekend," Dory offered with a cheery smile at Adam. "My treat."

"PULL OVER FOR A SEC," Adam said to Cait as they pedaled their bikes off the ferryboat and headed uphill onto Lopez Island the next morning.

He drew a pocket-size bike route book out of the saddlebag strapped to his bike and opened it to the section on rides in the San Juan islands.

"'Lopez Island,'" he read aloud, "'is a bicyclist's paradise. The—'"

"Or hell on wheels if you're not a bike freak," Cait interrupted. She eyed the incline ahead with a glum eye, knowing she must sound cranky and petulant. But she couldn't lighten the gloomy cloud that had already begun to darken her usually sunny disposition that morning. She heaved a helpless mental sigh. Exercise. The prospect of engaging in it brought out the worst in her every time. And despite her delight at being with Adam, today was no exception.

"Let me finish," Adam chided her, and read on. "'The hill from the ferry dock is the hard part. Beyond that the terrain is moderate. The route winds on isolated country roads through miles of rolling pastureland.'"

Cait pursed her lips. "I'll believe it when I see it."

"'Cumulative elevation gain is a gentle one thousand to two thousand feet.'"

"Gentle, my tush." Cait tapped a toe and glanced at the hill ahead. "Not if it's all in the first quarter mile, it isn't."

Adam chuckled and went on. "'In autumn the weather is often cool, clear and sunny.'"

Cait squinted up at the sun blazing in a blue sky. "Chalk up one for the guidebook. Up to now, I'd have sworn you were reading fairy tales."

Adam's chuckle rumbled into rich, ripe laughter. "I love it when you talk dirty."

"This is no laughing matter, Adam."

"For me it is. Whether it's cookies or cats or complaints, you tickle my funny bone every time."

"It's no joke. Fiction or nonfiction, two thousand feet is not amusing." But she couldn't help grinning as she grumped, for she loved it, too, making him laugh, hearing the happy sound, seeing the flash of ready humor in his green eyes.

"Maybe not, but the lady certainly is," he said, chuckling.

"Find something for the lady to laugh about at the top of that hill, then. She's going to need *something* to ease the pain."

"Just take it easy and you'll be all right," he said soothingly, his eyes still dancing.

"Don't I just wish."

Cait folded her arms across her chest and ruefully contemplated the hill ahead. It was nothing less than a Swiss Alp. Easy for Mr. Fitness with a capital *F* to scale. But a bet was a bet. The thing to do was to think of it as a challenge. She set her jaw as firmly as she could. If he could lick a plate clean at Euphoria, she could make it up that hill. She hoped.

"It's about seven miles to Dory's place," said Adam as he consulted the map in the book. He cleared his throat. "We can rest up and, um, have lunch there. Okay?"

He noticed that Cait had to clear her throat twice to his once before she could squeeze out an intelligible affirmative. He noticed further that once they were on their bikes and headed uphill, her handlebars wobbled as if she, too, might have had the place on the brain ever since the key had landed in his hand.

As for his brain, it was still working overtime on the possibilities inherent in Dory's blithe invitation. A bottle of fine wine, the soft lap of waves on the beach, Cait all his at last. He pulled ahead of her, unable to take the tantalizing sight of her luscious, rounded bottom any longer. A minute more of bringing up the rear and he'd be unable to scale an anthill.

So why didn't you just come out and say the beach house might be nice for more than just lunch? Cait admonished herself as she pedaled hard to keep up with Adam. But she knew why. She didn't want to sound as expectant as she felt. After all, she had been the one with the reservations about getting serious.

When she had told Dory they did nothing but rehearse those nights at his house, it was the truth. Adam had stuck to his word. He had said he'd wait until Cait was ready and he'd waited.

Whatever he might have wanted to do during their sedate rehearsals, it had gone undone. Not a touch, not a kiss. At first, Cait had respected him for it and for his understanding that she was not an impulsive person in matters of the heart. She had also had a wonderful time with him during those rehearsals, talking and laughing and learning steadily more about what a nice guy he was, so different from the superstar image his famous name carried with it.

Accompanying the respect, though, was the torture of privately wanting more than just talk. Knowing she could have said the word at any time and ended the torment made it all the harder. Cautious Cait, she knew, wasn't a description her sage father had just plucked out of thin air. But caution had finally given way to decision halfway through a Friday night of cleaning her apartment and trying to smooth things over with Truffles.

She'd picked up the phone and dialed Adam. Dory was right. It was time she caught up with the times and did herself a favor. She would invite him over. She had stood it long enough. His phone had rung fifteen times before she'd hung up and scowled her frustration at Truffles.

Cait had been left to console herself with a bag of Hershey's Kisses and a peeved cat who wasn't about to forgive her mistress for being a stranger most of the week. Small comfort when it was not chocolate Cait craved but Adam, day and night. Never had she felt such an emotional and physical hunger for a man as she had come to feel for him in that week.

"How's the seat, by the way?" he called back to her now as he pulled farther ahead. "Comfy enough for you?"

"Mhmph," Cait replied, hard pressed at that moment to find much comfort in anything but the presence of that key in Adam's pocket. Certainly there was none in the fit of her bottom to the seat of the bike Adam had loaned her. Yet one more indication of his sterling character was the foam-padded seat cover he'd supplied for her greater comfort. If only it felt as padded as it looked.

Oh, well. She tucked her chin down and switched to the sleek ten-speed's lowest gear, determined not to let the uphill grade from the ferry dock get the best of her. Much as she loathed physical exertion, she wasn't going to fall flat on her face today with Adam. A bet was a bet. And somewhere ahead was the beach house—and lunch.

From behind Cait heard the thump-thump of cars unloading off the ferry ramp. Glancing back, she discovered she had barely advanced a hundred yards. Already she was sweating as if she'd traversed an entire continent. On second thought, she amended, maybe falling flat on her face wouldn't be so bad. It couldn't be worse than this.

Looking forward again, she watched the distance between herself and Adam lengthen. She tried to distract herself with the riveting view she had of his tight buttocks flexing ahead of her. She tried to think about how his snug, navy sweat suit hugged every masculine contour of his body.

Hard as she tried, however, all she could think of at that moment was the number of feet in a mile. Multiplied by seven, those thousands equaled unmitigated agony. Beads of sweat rolled down her back under her lavender sweat suit, making her wish she had worn shorts and a halter. Good Lord, what had she gotten herself into with that bet? Already her tender tush, calves and thighs begged for mercy. As for her lungs, she was suddenly wishing she had half a dozen instead of just two.

Remember how nice Adam is, she told herself as she fell farther behind. *And charming. More charm per gorgeous square inch than any man you've ever known. Nice, charming and patient, too.*

And remember the Cuisinart you'll regain fair and square. Remember you can't afford to buy a replacement. Remember that pileup of bills at home and your landlord who's just about ready to evict you.

Perspiration popped out on her upper lip and forehead. It trickled in itchy little rivulets down her rib cage and between her breasts. In her heaving chest her laboring heart swelled like a giant blood vessel ready to burst.

Several more minutes of relentless torture found her reminded only of the fact that this was all Adam's doing. Nice? Him? Now she couldn't quite remember what had fostered that particular illusion. If not for him, she would never have put bottom to bike seat. If not for him, she wouldn't be huffing and puffing harder by the minute. Where was the charm in a man who'd do this to a fellow human being?

Though a tiny voice inside answered that he'd done it to ensure seeing more of her, she ignored it. She glared ahead at his receding figure and wondered as she gasped for air how she could have thought him anything but impossible. Him. It could only have been temporary insanity.

Cait groaned a little as every corpuscle in her body screamed for relief. Why had he picked on *her*? Why not Samantha Leotardo? Why Cait Rafferty when it was obvious anyone in the sweat set would have sacrificed the last ankle warmer on earth to ride rings around Lopez Island with Adam Webster?

The stream of traffic from the ferry passed on Cait's left, adding exhaust fumes to the air she gulped in by the lungful. A rusty, ancient Ford pickup rattled past. Keep On Truckin' a sticker on its venerable bumper encouraged. Cait gritted her teeth and hoped to someday run into whoever had conceived that suddenly insufferable slogan—preferably head-on with a Mack truck.

She squinted ahead to where Adam had now topped the rise of the hill and dropped out of sight. Her fingers tightened around the handlebars as an old memory surfaced. How many times had Doug pulled ahead like that on a long run, leaving her gasping behind? Too many to count. She could hear him now shouting back to her, "Get the lead out, Rafferty! No pain, no gain!"

Cait squeezed her eyes shut for an instant against the question that continued to prick at her. Adam was interested in her—there was no question of that. But why? Sure, they had a love of cats in common and laughed at the same things. Yes, the chemistry between them sparked in all the right ways. Did it ever!

But was he interested in her for just what she was, or for something else besides? He was a fitness guru, after all, and had been one before the bypass made fitness a life-or-death matter for him.

How did she know he wasn't seeking another convert in her? Lord knows a plump, sedentary chocoholic would be a prime candidate if he relished that sort of challenge. Was that it? Was he sneaking an exercise regimen in through the back door on her? Was this the first step in a soft-sell campaign to make her over?

Just beyond the crest of the hill Adam pulled over to wait for Cait. "Easy, fella," he muttered to himself. It *would* be easier if just thinking about her didn't do what it did to him. The only way he'd gotten up the hill was by forcing himself to pretend. *Pretend the late morning sunlight glinting in her hair doesn't take your breath away. Pretend she isn't wearing lavender sweats that make her look so soft and curvy you get hard just looking at her. Do yourself a favor.*

He slipped his sweatshirt off and stowed it in the saddlebag with the book and the water bottle. Either it was hot for this time of year or it was Cait who made it seem that way. He glanced down at the scar on his chest and remembered her fingers touching it that night by the fire.

A little less than seven miles to go. He sighed, leaned his bike against the rail fence that bordered the road and walked back to the crest of the hill to make sure she was all right.

If Cait had been able to spare a breath, it would have caught in her throat at the sight of him silhouetted above her. As it was, the best she could do was blink in astonished disbelief. He was waiting for her! Just when she had concluded he was the same kind of insensitive clod Doug had been, there he was, waiting for her. Running downhill to meet her, even.

"Hi, beautiful," he said when he reached her. "Need a little help from a friend?"

When she nodded breathlessly, he planted one hand on the frame of her bike and the other flat on her backside and literally pushed her up the last stretch. At the top he helped her off the bike.

"So hot," she said, gasping, as she fanned the fabric of her sweatshirt against her chest.

"Hold still for a sec." He pressed his fingers against the racing pulse at her throat, consulted his watch and then frowned. "Why didn't you get off and walk the bike up the hill if your heart rate was this high?"

Cait shook her head. "We bet on a bike ride, not a walk. Remember?"

"Cait," Adam said, brushing back the damp auburn wisps plastered to her forehead, "I thought you were at least halfway up to this. Get off and walk from now on if you can't breathe or if you feel overheated. Okay?"

He led her over to the fence and leaned against it with her until her chest stopped heaving. "Okay?" he repeated softly.

She lifted her eyes to meet his concerned gaze and nodded. He wasn't like Doug at all. Drill sergeant Doug had never waited for her or given her a helpful boost up a hill. The realization brought a wobbly smile from her at the sight of Adam's bare chest.

"Looks like I'm not the only one who got over-heated. Weren't you fully clothed when I last saw you?"

He grinned down at her. "Can't a guy work on his tan if he feels like it?"

What he was working hardest on was reining in a raging desire to pull her into his arms right there on the side of the road. She looked deliciously flushed from her uphill exertions. Just the way he had so many times imagined she would look after making love.

Patience, man. He turned away from the temptation and gazed out over the miles of fenced pastureland and graveled country road that awaited them.

Cait turned, too, and surveyed the landscape with a sigh of relief. "Flat. Chalk up another one for the guidebook."

Adam smiled down at her. "Think you can handle the flats with a few rest stops along the way?"

Cait returned the smile and murmured, "Sure. No sweat." Rest stops. Not at all like Doug. Her smile trembled. Doug who? Suddenly she couldn't remember. Downhill from where she and Adam stood she heard the ferry signal its departure.

AT THE TURNOFF to the cabin, Adam dismounted and held out the water bottle. Cait got off next to him and drank long and deeply. The day had unexpectedly turned into an Indian-summer scorcher, making her wish she could peel off her perspiration-soaked sweat-shirt as Adam had.

Seemingly oblivious to the heat, a red-tailed hawk soared overhead, uttering a gull-like cry. Cait stood in the circular shade of the stop sign, shielded her eyes with her hand and followed its swooping flight. In the grassy pastures on either side of the road cattle lowed as they grazed.

Adam drained the bottle, capped it and leaned back against the post of the stop sign. "You okay?"

She flexed her stiff calves. "A little sore, I guess, but better than I expected."

"Sore? Where?"

"Guess."

"I can't imagine." A teasing light danced into his eyes. "Where?"

She giggled. "Don't be dense."

"Look, if you'll be needing a massage anytime soon, I think I should know precisely where to start. Hmm, let's see now. Where could it be?" His gaze turned downright impudent and traveled from the tip of her sunburned nose to her parted lips. "There?" It dropped to her shoulders. "Or there?" It slid down to the curve of her breasts. He cleared his throat. "Or . . ."

Cait felt her nipples harden as if he'd touched his lips to them instead of only his gaze. "Adam—"

His eyes darkened and the teasing light died as they continued slowly down to her rounded hips. "Where, Cait? Wherever it hurts, I'll make it better."

Cait felt sure he sensed the meltdown taking place where his gaze was focused. Now that he had seen her unmistakable response to him against the damp front of her sweatshirt, how could he fail to sense everything she was feeling?

He raised his eyes, deep green and hypnotic in their intensity, to hers again. After a moment he bent his knee and braced the sole of his foot back flat against the signpost. Tiny erotic chills chased each other along Cait's spine as she realized the shift was to mask his own physical response to the moment.

"Believe it or not," he said in a thick voice, "I know my way around sore muscles. Masuo's been giving me lessons in shiatsu, Japanese massage. I just had one last night."

"So that's where you were." Cait couldn't hide the sudden bright note of relief in her voice. It hadn't been easy to forget the Samanthas and their postcards with the phone numbers. It hadn't been easy to convince herself he wasn't out with one of them.

"You tried to call?"

She nodded. "I . . . changed my mind last night. I wanted to see you."

There was a long, pendant pause before he asked softly, "Why?"

"Because I—" She swallowed hard and took a tentative step toward him. "I decided you were right about time being precious and not wasting it."

He didn't say anything. His eyes just got darker and darker and then he dropped the water bottle and held his arms open to her.

With a faint moan Cait stepped forward into his embrace. He wrapped her tightly against him, and she felt her heart dive, swoop and soar like the wild bird she had watched on high.

"Oh, Adam," she whispered into the damp heat of his bare chest. "This has been the longest week of my life."

"Mine, too, sweetheart, mine, too."

Until that moment Cait hadn't known what a potent sexual stimulant a man's honest sweat could be. She pressed her face into the moist dark hair on his chest and breathed deeply of his musky scent. He smelled of hot sun and salt, virile and male. She parted her lips against him and tasted all of that and more.

Behind her his hands slipped up under the ribbed bottom of her sweatshirt and flattened against her bare back to pull her closer. The coaxing movement molded her hips into the cradle formed by his flexed knee, and Cait felt in no uncertain terms what he had tried to conceal.

Up, up his kneading fingers moved, beyond the band of her bra to her shoulder blades. Finally, he thought. Patience and perseverance had finally paid off. Her skin was as hot and damp as his, her breathing as ragged, her heart as wild in her chest.

"Cait," he murmured into her hair, "we have to do something about this really soon."

"I know." She lifted her face to look at him and shivered when his thumbs brushed around her sides, to where her breasts softly swelled. "That's why we're going to take Dory up on that invitation—if it's all right with you."

"All right with me? Are you kidding? Can't you feel how all right that would be with me?"

"Yes." Cait pressed her hips more tightly against his.

"You're sure this is what you want, Cait?"

"Yes."

He closed his eyes and pulled in a deep breath as if he couldn't quite believe his ears. "And you'll respect me in the morning?"

"I'll even bring you breakfast in bed."

His eyes opened in a blaze of green, and as the final word left her lips, Cait lifted them to his. It was a kiss as elemental and blatantly sensual as the scent that emanated from his skin, and Cait drank it in like life itself.

His mouth was hot and wet, his invading tongue a licking flame lighting fires in her that burned hotter with each welcome invasion. Her fingernails dug into the bunched muscles of his bare shoulders as she crushed her mouth and body to him with a hunger that matched his.

Surely, she thought, his back would be marked with the vertical imprint of that signpost forever, just as the scar would mark his chest for all time. Just as the feel of his hips pressing his need into the hollow of hers would survive in her body's memory as long as she lived. Nor would she ever forget the fierce tug in her womb as his thumbs slipped into the cups of her bra and massaged her sensitized nipples to hard buds of ecstasy.

So loud was the thundering of her heart in her ears that she would never have heard the engine had it not backfired as it approached the stop. She jerked apart from Adam when the sound split the air. He groaned as she spun away, and hitched his roadside knee several inches higher.

The old farmer in the ancient Ford pickup Cait had seen earlier tipped his billed cap as he clattered to a stop.

"Big haystack up the road a piece, sonny," he called out the window to Adam. He smiled a kindly, sympathetic smile. "Nice and private."

"Uh, thanks," Adam replied.

"Glad to oblige." The man tipped his hat again in a jaunty goodbye. Cait and Adam exchanged an abashed glance and watched the old jalopy rattle off in a cloud of exhaust and dust. Keep On Truckin', the rear bumper sticker advised in farewell.

When the dust settled, Adam gave her a roguish smile and tipped his own imaginary hat. "Well, ma'am," he drawled, "where do we truck to first? The haystack or Dory's place?"

She lifted an appraising eyebrow at his angled knee. "Whichever is closer, sonny."

HE EMITTED a low, appreciative whistle fifteen minutes later when they rode to the end of a winding driveway and the house on the low sea bluff came into view.

"If this is Dory's idea of a weekend place, I'd like to see where she lives the other five days," Adam commented with a wry laugh.

Cait nodded. "I thought it would be more of a cabin." Except for the natural cedar exterior, though, there was nothing rustic about it. It was all skylights and clean angles, architect-designed to resemble a natural extension of the bluff.

They parked their bikes on the flagstone walk and entered through a burled redwood door. Huge windows faced west from the main living area to frame a deep blue slice of the San Juan Channel. Nature had been invited indoors with a generous use of wood and natural fibers.

The furnishings were a casual blend of earth tones spiced with cinnamon and burnt orange. A glass top transformed a swirl of driftwood into a dramatic cocktail table. The soft carpet reminded Cait so much of sun-warmed sand that she pulled off her shoes and socks and sank her toes in it. Adam shucked out of his, too, and they grinned at each other like children on a beach.

The kitchen to one side was long and narrow like a boat galley. Up an open staircase they found two loft bedrooms, one larger with a king-size bed, the other with twins. Each room had its own skylight, bath and view of the channel. In one open closet hung a cluster of terry bathrobes in a variety of colors and sizes.

"My kind of place. No phone, no TV, just us and nobody else." Adam flopped down on his back in the square of sunlight that washed the king-size bed in buttery warmth. He patted the quilted bedspread at his side. "Come here, beautiful."

Cait hovered in the doorway and glanced dubiously down at her sweat-splotched lavender sweatshirt. "This is not my idea of beautiful," she said, curling her bare toes in sudden shyness into the carpet. "I need a shower."

"You need a kiss first and so do I."

"I'm all, uh, damp and perspiry."

"You're not the only one. Come, Cait."

She moved over to the bed, and he pulled her down to lie beside him. Then he levered himself up on one elbow and gazed into her eyes without touching her, without speaking. Outside Cait could hear the plaintive cries of sea gulls, the faint slap and swish of waves on the beach below. Inside there was only the sound of breathing, hers and Adam's.

They lay like that for a few silent minutes that were more eloquent than speech for what was communicated across the short span of their locked gazes.

"You're quite a woman, Cait Rafferty," Adam finally whispered.

She lifted her fingertip to trace the dark, winged shape of his eyebrow. "You're quite something yourself," she whispered back.

"Mmm. Repeat that, please." He moved his head to coax her finger to his lips.

She obeyed, punctuating each word with the soft press of her index finger into his full lower lip. When he opened his mouth and drew it in to the first joint, she felt the silky stroke of his tongue all the way to her toes. His lips released her and moved with soft words against her moistened skin. "Say my name again."

She whispered it with a catch of breath at the amazing sensations his merest touch could evoke in her. For he was caressing her hand now, tracing the shape of her fingers with his, lazily examining them in the sunlight that streamed down, cupping her palm to his lips to press a soft kiss into it.

Cait watched him with a mixture of awe and wonder. To her they were just her hands. The short-nailed, capable-looking hands of a working cook. For Adam, though, they seemed to be the most magical of appendages, worthy of adoring with tiny kisses that covered every square inch of their surface and made her wonder how it would feel to be kissed all over like that.

"Mmm, for someone all damp and perspiry you sure smell nice. Like you did at the stop sign. Lord, what a moment . . ."

"I remember," she replied in a breathy whisper.

"I wanted you so much right then. Just the way you were." He flicked his tongue against her wrist. "I want you even more right now."

She plucked weakly with her other hand at her sweatshirt. "Like this?"

"Like this."

Cait felt his tongue savor her skin again and she gasped, "Adam . . ."

He looked straight into her eyes. "I don't think I can wait through a shower."

"Neither can I," she said quickly.

With a long, slow sigh of obvious relief at her reply, he reached out and pulled her flush against his bare chest. Her fingers curled into the damp hair there, and he knew there had never been even a question in her mind about waiting. Then she gave her mouth to him in a moaning kiss that was a mix of surrender and invitation, and he knew nothing would stop this, short of that old Ford pickup backfiring up the stairs and into the loft.

But he hadn't forgotten Cait's earlier admission that her ex-fiancé had not wooed her with words. God knows what else the poor fool hadn't done, Adam told himself.

With that in mind he clamped down on his own raging need and vowed to make love to Cait as if she were the virgin she had been before Doug.

Cait felt the intensity of his kiss soften to a sweet yearning. His lips went loose and moist on hers as he slid his tongue over and around hers.

"Come to me, Cait," he whispered into her mouth. Slowly and deliberately he continued the gentle oral parry and thrust until her hips imitated the same sliding motion against his. "Yes, that's it."

To Cait, it seemed that his hands moved lightly over her everywhere at once. Even as the fingers of one hand laced through her sun-dappled hair, the fingers of the other brushed down the soft column of her throat to caress one breast and then the other.

"I want to see you," he whispered. He slipped the sweatshirt over her head, fighting for control. The smoky look she gave him when it came off was no help. He had to press her back onto the bed and bury his face in the moist heat between her confined breasts to escape it. No escape had ever been as sweet or as ineffective.

"Adam, *please*." Cait wound her fingers in his dark hair to raise his head from her. Then she unclasped the lavender bra she had worn for him and peeled the lace cups back. "Touch me, kiss me," she urged. "Please."

He gazed first, then touched, cupped her creamy fullness in his hand and stroked a trembling thumb over her pale auburn nipple.

"Beautiful," he whispered. "And don't ask this time if I really mean it. You have beautiful breasts, Cait. And the same goes for your hair and eyes and skin. So smooth, so soft. Does this feel good, sweet?" He rotated his thumb in an erotic circle on her. "Tell me."

"Oh, yes," she gasped. "And does this to you?" she inquired in turn as her fingertips feathered through his chest hair and found a pebbled nipple of their own.

"More than good," he growled. He touched his mouth to her and sucked gently at first, then harder as her touch quickened his flesh to a tiny point of pure pleasure.

"Don't stop, Adam . . ."

"I won't if you won't," he breathed, plying his lips and tongue on each breast in turn until she whimpered and moved her hands down from his chest to pluck at the waistband of his sweatpants.

"Not yet," he murmured. "I want this to be so special for you, sweetheart."

"It already is," she protested weakly. "I've never felt so—"

"Sh. I've been thinking about being with you like this too long to let it be over too soon." He slid a gentle hand down to slip her sweatpants off.

She lifted her hips for him to remove the panties that matched her bra, but found herself thwarted when he gently pressed her back into the mattress. He pushed himself up to rest on one elbow beside her and traced the elastic at her hip, inching ever inward to where thigh and torso converged.

Cait held her breath, craving his more intimate touch. Her eyes followed his heavy-lidded gaze down to where her thighs shifted to invite that touch. She wondered what that intent gaze meant. Did he think the generous flare of her hips and thighs as worthy of the word "beautiful" as her hair and eyes and breasts? Or was he thinking, as Doug had grown to think, that a woman who measured 38-32-40 with a little cellulite thrown in was fertile ground for improvement?

Cait closed her eyes against the thought. She didn't want to wonder. Not now. Not when his fingers were parting her thighs, tracing up and down the silken delta between them. It was hard enough to think straight, much less wonder such disturbing things. It was enough to feel what he was making her feel right now, this minute.

"Is this what you want, Cait?" he asked in a husky undertone.

"Yes . . ." she sighed as he increased the length and pressure of his erotic caress and returned his mouth to her breast. "You could drive me very crazy doing that, Adam."

"I want to. I want you to know how crazy I've felt all week. When we rehearsed those nights without even a good-night kiss. Unbearable."

"Don't you think I felt it, too? I feel it *now*, Adam. What more do you want?" she pleaded, arching to the warm, kneading heel of his palm.

"You could touch me like I'm touching you, for a start, babe."

Her eyes locked to his, she slid a hand under his waistband, found his hard warmth, stroked his thick smoothness from base to velvety tip and gloried in hearing him echo her gasp of delight. When he could take no more, he halted her hand with his and rose from the bed to strip off his sweatpants and briefs.

Sunlight streamed down from overhead, burnishing the ripple of muscles under his skin with his every movement. Cait watched, fascinated, as he straightened and paused for a moment in half sun and shade. He was every inch a man, she thought, her gaze drawn from the tapered pattern of hair on his stomach down to the magnificent measure of his desire for her.

"Now you, sweetheart," he murmured, leaning over to slide her panties off. Then he was beside her again, his mouth devouring hers, his hand guiding hers to his straining hardness, his fingers parting her sun-warmed thighs again to delve into the soft auburn down to her femininity.

Cait had never felt so cherished, so adored in her life. His touch was as yearning and gently searching as his tongue against hers. He sought and found her tenderest, most intimate response, and Cait gasped her pleasure into his mouth with each sweet, unfurling stroke of his fingers at the heart of her passion.

"Oh, God, Cait . . . I knew you'd be like this, ready for everything I want to give you."

"Adam, please—stop—don't stop—I'm going to—"

"It's all right. Go with it."

"But I've never—"

"Honey, when I said special, I meant it. Let me make it that way for you this first time. Yes?"

"Ohhh, yes . . ." Her fingers left him to dig into the bedspread. Her thighs fell farther apart. Desperately she arched her hips upward to the ever greater pleasure of his touch. Dipping inside on each downstroke, he increased the erotic tempo to an electrifying rhythm that rocketed through her heart.

"Oh, God . . . Adam . . ."

"Let it come, sweet."

Her breath came in sharp little pants as her surrender to his whispered pleas lifted her ever higher until she climaxed, her breath coming in long, shuddering gasps.

"Ah, Cait," he whispered when she drifted back down to the golden glow of reality. "Now that was special."

Cait squeezed her thighs together where his hand still claimed her. "But you haven't—"

"I will. And you will, too, sweet. All over again." Adam brushed her lips with a feathery kiss and lazily resumed his sensual stroking.

"I don't know. I've never—"

"You'll have it, sweetheart. Everything."

"Ohhh, Adam." Cait sucked in a breath as the spell of his touch wove over and into her again, warm and sinuous like slow fire in her veins. She felt his hardened manhood press against her hip and reached out to feather a seeking caress that aroused her just as much as his touches.

To further inflame her, he whispered into her ear everything he intended to do, punctuating each word with a velvet flick of his tongue against her earlobe. Silently he thanked his stars that she was as sensually responsive as he had suspected she might be. He could never have lasted this long had she not been such a joy to please that he lost all thought of himself in the pleasing.

"Now, Adam—all of you this time," she demanded a little later in a whisper thick with the honey of a renewed desire.

She was slick and ready when he settled between her legs, and so tight his control almost deserted him. Inch by slow inch he eased deeper and deeper until Cait wrapped her legs around him and urged him home to the hilt.

Locked in the age-old embrace, they moved together. This time it was Cait who whispered soft words of encouragement and coaxed him into the long plunging thrusts that propelled him faster, faster, higher to the final surge when he reached the end of control.

His deep racking spasms triggered her second climax, one that so completed her and so merged her body with his that it left her weak with joy and awe. In the aftermath she dazedly lay in the sun-drenched cradle of Adam's arms and knew the proverb hanging above her stove had just been proven wrong.

Nothing on earth was sweeter than loving Adam.

OR SO SHE THOUGHT until Adam romanced her that evening with fine wine and firelight after a steamy shower together. And made slow, drowsy love to her yet again when they woke the next morning.

It was after that, when they were both still basking in the afterglow, that he popped the question.

"Would you collaborate on a book with me, sweet?"

"Do what?"

"Collaborate on my third book. I'm writing it now."

"I'm a cook, Adam, not a jock."

"That's what I'm getting at. This book concentrates on more than just running. I want to include a chapter of recipes that are healthy, easy to fix and taste good. Unfortunately I don't know the first thing about cooking."

Cait sank back into the rumpled sheets and stared at him. "Have you forgotten I'm first and foremost a *chocolate* cook?"

"Dory says you cook a mean fettuccine." He shrugged. "You took to making sushi like Masuo takes to karate. All week we've put together just the sort of things my publisher and I want in the book and look at the fan mail."

"True, but— I don't know, Adam. Where would I find the time? I still have the show three days a week and a schedule of classes at the store."

"What if I offered you an immediate advance on royalties that made it worth your while to quit the classes on the off days?"

That silenced her into suddenly giving it more serious consideration. If there was one thing she was desperate for, it was the rent and the car payments.

"Look, I couldn't avoid overhearing that conversation you had with your editor a few nights ago," Adam added. "It sounded like a replay of the one I had with mine before *Runner's High* came out."

Cait stared at him. "You had overdue rent, too?"

"Yep. I had more financial valleys than peaks before the book, believe me. I know what it's like to scrape the bottom of the barrel for cash and come up empty. You didn't think I was born a millionaire author, did you?"

"I don't know. I actually haven't had much time in the past week to think about it, I guess. How *did* you start out?"

"On a dairy farm. When I was fifteen, Dad died and it was all up to me and Mom. We worked the place together, milking morning and night year in, year out." He smiled a little. "Cows never go on vacation."

Cait smiled, too. "No, they're too busy keeping Milk Duds on the candy shelves. How did you end up writing a book about running instead of cows?"

"How did *you* end up writing a book about chocolate?"

"Easy. I love to look at it, smell it, eat it and cook it."

"Same with me and running. You see, I never went to college because Mom could never have handled the herd alone. My whole life was dairy farming—by necessity, not choice. For years after I graduated from high school, I continued to farm, but my heart wasn't really in it. To be honest, I didn't know what I wanted to be, but I did know it wasn't what I was.

"I started running to release my frustrations, I guess. My doctor said it was a good thing, since heart disease runs in families. The neighbors thought I was nuts, of course, in those days. Just shook their heads. Embarrassed Mom so much she almost put me up for adoption even though I was a grown man."

He chuckled and rolled over on his back, lacing his fingers behind his head. "Crazy thing was, it made me feel a lot better. Cheered me up, gave me more energy, made me feel I was doing something good for myself. I'd go for a run after my morning and evening milking, and when I got back, I didn't hate cows so much."

"Where did you find time to write?"

"Here and there at first. Running made me feel so good that I started writing about it in a personal journal I kept. Then the bull stepped on my foot and broke it and I ended up in a cast clear up to my a—er, hip for six months. Mom and I mortgaged ourselves to the hilt to hire a man to replace me, and while he worked, I wrote the first definitive book on running and sent it to New York. The rest is history."

"Just like that?" Cait raised herself on an elbow. "It sold to a publisher first time out?"

"Bingo."

"Lucky you," Cait said with a teasing scowl. "Mine got rejected ten times before it finally sold."

"Ah, but how many copies of yours are they printing?"

"Twenty-five thousand."

"Not bad for an unknown. Mine drew a whopping first print run of ten thousand. As my mother said more often than she needed to, 'Who on earth wants to read a book about running? Only weirdos like you, son.'

Like Mom, the publisher figured there'd be only enough weirdos out there to make it worth a two-thousand-dollar advance."

"But it sold millions."

Adam nodded and grinned. "Yep. It was the right book at the right time and threw everyone for a loop, including me. Paid the hired hand, too."

"Does your mom still live on the farm?"

"You bet." His grin widened. "With the hired hand, who's now my stepfather. Mom lucked out, too. The place is doing pretty well, considering the plight of most farmers these days."

"Amazing. And you've never had to look a cow in the eye since?"

"Nope." His grin faded slightly. "Not since wealth and fame caught up with me. But I still wake up in the morning sometimes, thinking I've overslept and the udders are ready to explode. Then I remember I've written two books with a third one on the way—one you're going to do the recipes for, I hope."

She curled into his arms, which he held out to her, and sighed in confusion. "There are a lot of diet cooks out there who know more about calories and carbohydrates than I ever will."

"You said it yourself on one of the shows—if you can cook it and like it, so can anyone else. And as Dory says, you and I are a dynamite team. If we went on tour together with our 'opposites attract' act, we'd sell so many books you'd never have to worry about the rent again."

"Now there's a thought."

"Entertain it, sweet."

"Well all right," she reluctantly agreed. "But that's all I'm promising. This could get complicated, you know. Jeremy—my editor—has said more than once that collaboration is like marriage. A major disagreement can end up in divorce."

"Sweetheart, we've been engaged in the ultimate collaboration here for hours without one word of discord."

"Hmm, you *do* have a point there."

"That's not all I have."

"Adam, are you—? Oh, Adam, you are. Again."

"I can't help it. There's something about being in a bed naked with you that makes a wild man out of me."

"Hmm, I'm beginning to feel a little primitive again myself."

"See what I mean, sweet? What could we possibly find to disagree about after this?" Adam murmured, capturing her mouth in a deep, erotic kiss that made her dizzily wonder the same thing.

8

WHAT COULD THEY POSSIBLY find to disagree about? The answer would surely never be found between the sheets. Cait's cheeks flushed as she reflected on that fact three weeks after Lopez.

She stood in front of Adam's stove concocting the first recipe for his new book, knowing it wasn't the heat from the burner that elicited her abashed reaction. It was the joyous memory of what had taken place upstairs in his bed during numerous nights since that weekend on the island.

"Meow," commented Mordecai from atop the refrigerator, where he watched like a hawk for the tiniest spill that might need licking up.

Three echoes of the same sentiment issued from Mitchell, Mollie and Truffles, who sat, each on a kitchen stool, watching Cait cook. Cait was still amazed at how welcome she and Truffles had become as weekend guests at Adam's house.

"Pipe down, you guys," she chided. "I'm thinking. And I'm warning you, what I'm cooking is hot stuff."

She swished a wire whisk dreamily through the low-fat Tarragon Cheese Sauce she was experimenting with. Was it love? Whatever it was, it made her heart and limbs tremble whenever she thought of Adam, whenever she touched him, whenever their bodies fed each other's hunger with a passion so great it could only briefly be sated.

Disagree in that respect? Never.

Disagree in other respects? Cait's eyebrows drew together in a frown of concentration. Now, that was a different matter. It wasn't that they disagreed, exactly. To be truly exact, she didn't know what to call it.

"Want to walk down to the lake and feed the ducks?" Adam would ask if they ended up at his place on a Saturday or Sunday afternoon.

It was the way he posed it that left Cait stymied for a single answer to the question. No, walking wasn't her style. On the other hand, yes, she wanted to feed the ducks with Adam. She loved to stand with him in the middle of a quacking multitude and toss out stale bread. Green Lake ducks, the greediest and noisiest in Seattle, were always good for more than a little hilarious laughter.

Laughing with Adam was enough of a trade-off that she walked without complaint. She couldn't help wondering, though, if it wasn't a subtle ploy to sucker her into exercise with the softest of soft sells.

"Let's drive down," she'd suggested once, just to see what would happen.

"Okay," he'd said after what seemed to her a measured moment, and they'd driven down to the lake and back.

It nagged at her, that elongated moment. Was it all her imagination? she wondered. Maybe. Once burned, twice shy? Probably. Still, the walks weren't the only thing Adam gave her to wonder about.

"Come in with me," he had invited once when she sat at the edge of the pool dangling her feet in the water as he finished his laps. "Water's nice and warm, sweet, and so am I."

"I hate swimming."

"Why?"

"Wouldn't you if you'd weighed two hundred pounds in high school? Suiting up was torture. To this day, I still hate the smell of chlorine."

"You don't tip two hundred on the scale now, Cautious Cait," he coaxed in that smooth, seductive way he had of forever charming her out of her inhibitions.

"Even so, ankle-deep's more my style," she'd countered. "Besides, I'm not dressed for it. Jeans and a sweatshirt aren't swimming gear."

"You could take it all off." He swam close and wrapped a hand around her ankle. "No one can see, just me." He clasped her other ankle and slid both hands up her calves to where her jeans were rolled to the knee.

Cait reached her hands out to his shoulders to playfully ward him off and found herself just as playfully tumbled forward.

"Beast!" she shrieked, and an instant later she was in his arms in the water. It wasn't quite as warm as promised, but *he* was. Warmer than warm.

Now Cait idled her whisk in the sauce and flushed hotter and deeper as she recalled how her waterlogged clothes had peeled off as readily as the skin off a ripe peach. The inhibitions she'd shed in that pool! Just thinking about it sent shivers of longing through her for more to shed.

Would she ever get enough of the man? she wondered. *Never*, a tiny voice deep inside answered. She frowned again. That was the trouble. As things stood, she couldn't get enough physically, and that was clouding things emotionally. Emotionally she felt—what? *Crazy about him*, the tiny voice piped up again. All smiles whenever he was around. Effervescent. Passionate. Joyous. Filled to the brim with—

No. It was too soon for all-out love with no holds barred. Too much still hung in a too precarious balance. Cait deepened her frown and shook the yearning off. Certain things had to be remembered here. Such as how easily he had lured her into the lap pool on several occasions since that first one. She who had hated even the blue of the pool in days gone by.

Despite it, she had forgotten past embarrassments, past hurts and everything else in the pool with Adam. With him she had floated on waves of water-slicked ecstasy. With him she had even swum lazy half laps, lolled in his arms like a mermaid, *felt* like one, for heaven's sake.

Her. Cait Rafferty. Swimming. Walking twenty blocks round-trip to feed ducks. Going three weekends without a wake-up cigarette. Who, after all, needed any other eye-opener than Adam, who gently coaxed her out of her morning slumbers with a repertoire of drowsy caresses to satisfy her every drowsy desire? It was enough to disturb any self-respecting couch potato.

Disturbed anew as she thought about it, she whipped the sauce to velvet smoothness with a nervous energy it didn't require and then reached into the candy box on the counter for a chocolate-coated molasses chip to calm herself.

She closed her eyes and rolled the chip around in her mouth. Chocolate. What would she do without it? The cheese sauce might have to be low-fat, but the same, thankfully, didn't apply to the real stuff of life. That, at least, had not changed.

However, she decided after two more calming chips, life with Adam in it certainly could be sweeter than sweet. Everything else was coming up candy-coated, too. *Northwest Live* continued to gain viewers. Jeremy had called with the good news that *Chocolate à la Carte* was miraculously back on schedule and due in the bookstores any day. Adam's generous advance for the recipe chapter had paid the rent and the overdue bills for the time being.

As the third chip melted on her tongue, Cait only hoped she never had to choose between chocolate and Adam as she had once chosen between herself and Doug.

The front door opened, sending her eyes wide open, too, with eager anticipation. Adam was back early from his evening run around Green Lake. With flying fingers she tied on her Kiss the Cook apron over the denim peasant skirt and plaid blouse she wore.

"Aha!" he exclaimed when he came in. "Your wish is my command." He folded her into his arms against his sweaty gray sweats. "How's my chief collaborator?"

"Chief? Are there others?" she murmured, going weak as she always did at the feel of his body against hers.

"Only lesser others. Don't breathe a word of it to them, though." He glanced at the four felines, who looked on with immense interest.

Cait tipped her chin enticingly up to his. "If only you'd obey my apron, I wouldn't have a chance of breathing even a syllable."

He obeyed without further ceremony, making breathing, speaking and standing upright under her own power impossible for several sensational seconds. It was like this every time, she thought dazedly. He jogged in wearing sweats and sweat, and she took to his rich musky scent like Os took to Oreos.

"Lord, you taste like heaven," he mumbled against her lips, wondering if his instant response to her would ever lessen, hoping it never did. Where would he find another like Cait? Her sunny smile and ready laugh warmed his days. He could talk to her about so many things. Her innate appetite for the sensual, be it chocolate or the pleasures of his bed, warmed his nights. What, now, would he do without her in his life? He hated to even think about it.

"Adam Webster," she whispered in mock horror when she was finally able to break the kiss. "*What* is going on in those sweatpants of yours?"

"Come with me into the shower and wonder no more." He slid her skirt up her thighs and cupped her buttocks with his hands.

"Adam, really. Aren't you even the least bit worn out? How far did you run?" she inquired, dizzied by the swiftness with which she felt inclined to follow him anywhere, everywhere. Upstairs or down, in the pool or out, drenched with sweat or fresh from a shower. A kiss, a touch, and reality melted away.

"Not far enough," he replied. "Never far enough these days. I'm Adam Webster, remember? A very physical person as persons go."

"Hmm . . . yes, that you are. I can feel even now just how physical you are."

"You're not the only one."

She gave him a saucy smile. "You mean it shows?"

"Yes," he groaned, pulling her hips flush against his. "I can tell already this morning wasn't enough. Last night wasn't enough. Come upstairs, sweetheart."

⋆

"HAS IT OCCURRED to you we've been almost inseparable these past few weeks?" Adam murmured much later after his body and Cait's had sought and found temporary peace once more.

"It's . . . occurred to me," she said slowly.

He stroked her cheek with tender fingers. "I'm talking 'inseparable' meaning 'serious' meaning 'love,' Cait."

"I know. But it's only been a month, Adam."

"The voice of caution again." He levered himself up on an elbow and traced the shape of her eyebrow. "I knew it was the real thing the night you burned the cookies."

She stared at him. "You couldn't have. Not that soon."

"I did then and I do now. I love you, sweet, with all my heart—such as it is."

"Adam, you don't know what you're saying. You—"

"Who says? You're not the only one in love around here, lady."

"Me? I've never mentioned the word."

"Cait, your body speaks a language all its own. Only a woman in love gives herself the way you give yourself to me. Not that I wouldn't like to hear it in so many words." He settled a gaze on her that searched and compelled but couldn't quite elicit the admission from her blocked throat.

After a moment of discomfited silence on her part, he inquired, "What, Cait? What makes it so impossible for you to say the same thing out loud to me?"

She drew away, not altogether sure herself. "Love is . . . complicated. It doesn't happen overnight."

"It did to me."

"That's beside the point. Love leads to marriage, and if two people aren't headed in the same direction together, things fall apart."

"All right, let's talk marriage, then. As I've said before, I want to settle down, have a family, live the normal life I haven't lived in the past few years. I've gotten the feeling over the past few weeks you want the same thing."

Cait swallowed hard. "Adam, just because we want some of the same things doesn't mean we can make a go of it. I know."

"Cautious Cait again," Adam said with a cynical twist in his voice. "What in hell happened between you and what's-his-face that makes you so damn skittish about heading straight for what you want?"

Cait pulled completely away. "For one thing, he was a runner, like you. For another, he was a runner *because* of you, because of *Runner's High*."

"That's a fact," Adam said after a moment. "But so are a lot of people in this world. What makes him stand out from the crowd?"

"He was a nice, sweet guy before he bought the book, that's what."

"And after that?"

Cait gathered the sheet to her breasts and fought back the tears she had until now thought she was beyond shedding. "After that he headed in the opposite direction. In no time we were poles apart."

"What does that have to do with us?" His voice was deadly quiet, but he reached a warm hand out to cup the shoulder she had turned away from him. "Are you saying I'm like him, Cait?"

"Yes—no—I mean—" She sighed. "I don't know. For so long I've thought he was like *you*, his big hero. Then I met you and—"

"And?"

"What can I say? Here we are in bed together." She shook her head in confusion. "You're not exactly the arrogant superstar I thought you were at first. And you're not quite the . . . the firebrand Doug made you sound like."

"You mean he was the one who read the book and not you?"

"Yes. But you're not as opinionated as he made you sound."

"Opinionated about what?"

"Fitness, weight, body image. That sort of thing."

"I was before the bypass. But a thing like that can broaden a man's viewpoint a bit, I guess. Fitness is still important to me but for different reasons now." He tightened his grip on her shoulder. "Is that the problem, Cait? The bypass? The uncertain future I might seem to face because of it?"

She turned back to him with stricken eyes. "Oh, no, Adam. Not that. I never thought of it that way. I mean, you . . . well, you have the energy of a sixteen-year-old."

"Sixteen, huh?" His gaze warmed as his arm slipped around her and drew her back. "And just how many sex-crazed adolescents are you comparing me to, I'd like to know? Or am I being compared to that former fiancé of yours?"

"No," Cait insisted, unable to resist nestling into the broad curve of Adam's shoulder once again. "You know that's not the case."

"I know you loved him."

"Yes. Or maybe I just thought I did at the time."

"But he hurt you."

"We hurt each other."

"And you're afraid the same thing will happen again with me?"

"It could."

"And because of that you won't pull out all the stops where I'm concerned."

"I didn't say that."

"Cait, why can't you admit we're a match made in heaven? You, me, Libra, Aquarius, we're perfect."

"Aquarius?" She struggled halfway out of his arms. "You said you were a Scorpio."

"Oops. Does Scorpio rising count for anything on the truth meter? Come back here, sweet."

"You lied."

"I fibbed. And only to keep you warming up to me that day in Dory's office. What else could I do? You weren't buying stock in matches made in heaven that day."

"Even so—"

"Come here and get close again."

"Adam—" But she was softening already, warming again to him as he tugged her back into his arms. Finally she came of her own accord, willing to be mollified, willing to be held as only he could hold her.

"There," he said with pleasure when she was nestled against him once more. "Now, back to the subject of my body. Is that all you want me for?"

"Adam, you know the answer to that."

"Do I? You're awfully closemouthed tonight, sweet. Aren't you even a little bit in love? Not even ankle-deep in it?"

"I just can't dive in over my head yet, Adam. I'm sorry."

"Me, too, but I guess I can settle for body language for a while longer." He hauled her closer and draped a leg over hers. "Speak to me, Cait. When I'm stuck in a lonely hotel room next week, I want to remember every word."

"What hotel room?"

"I'm doing a seven-city tour to repromote my books. They keep selling enough to warrant it. My publicist in New York called with the itinerary this morning while you were in the shower. I leave a week from tomorrow."

"Next Sunday? Oh, Adam, how exciting!" Her head and shoulders shot up from the pillow.

Adam rolled his eyes in patent dismay. "San Francisco, L.A., Dallas, Kansas City, Chicago, Boston and the Big Apple crammed into five days is not exciting."

"To someone who's never been east of Walla Walla, it is." Cait propped her shoulders up against the headboard of the bed, her gray eyes sparkling.

"Not for me," he said. "I've regretted signing that promotion clause in the contract ever since my operation. But my name's on it, and a deal's a deal. I'm stuck."

"But San Francisco and Manhattan. Think of it!"

He rolled over flat on his back and flung an aggrieved forearm over his eyes. "I don't believe this. I bare my heart, and what do I get? Three little words in return? No. I say I'm leaving on a tour I could do without, and what do I get? A flood of tears because she'll miss me more than I know? Not a trickle."

"But of course I'll miss you," she protested, her tone shifting from excited to repentant. "Terribly."

"How terribly? In detail, please."

She slid back down to his level and trailed her lips along the inside of his forearm until he lifted it from his closed eyes. "Most terribly," she whispered, touching a soft kiss to each eyelid and then to his mouth. "Enough to wish I could come along so I wouldn't have to miss you at all."

He opened his eyes. "You'd come if you could?"

"Well, sure, but I can't. I have the show three days a week, remember? And we have cats to feed."

"Masuo will do it. He loves them."

"That doesn't solve the problem of the show." Cait bit her lip and thought for a moment. "Unless I could tape the segments beforehand."

"Do it," he said quickly. "I've been thinking we could leave on Saturday and have the weekend to ourselves before the rat race starts."

"You've been *thinking*? You've already given this some thought?"

"More than some. I've rehearsed it in my mind a million times." He heaved a mock-wounded sigh and stared heavenward. "I was going to ask you to come right after you said you loved me. But you didn't—so I didn't."

"Oh."

"But I'm a glutton for punishment, I guess. Come, Cait. And don't say you can't afford it, sweet, because *I* can."

Cait traced a fingertip thoughtfully down his cheek, along his jaw, to the hollow of his throat. "I'd have to talk to Dory first."

"Do it." He turned and pulled Cait urgently into his arms. "Call her. Talk her into it."

"Right now?"

"Yes. I mean, no." His voice lowered to a seductive growl. "Do it after you speak to me in that very special language one more time."

Cait let out a shivery sigh and drew her fingertip down from the quickening pulse at his throat to the scar on his chest. "I can't get used to it," she whispered. "This doesn't slow you down one bit, does it?"

"Not when you're around to speed things up."

"ANOTHER GLASS OF PERRIER before we land, Mr. Webster?" cooed the slim, blond flight attendant for what seemed to Cait the twentieth time during the Saturday-afternoon flight from Seattle to San Francisco.

Adam shook his head, smiled his diffident smile and declined as politely as he had the second time he had been asked.

Cait stifled an impatient sigh, smoothed the skirt of her apricot linen suit and mentally ground her teeth as the attendant hovered for a moment longer and then moved on. If it had slipped her mind in the weeks since his stint on *Northwest Live* that Adam was who he was, Cait was firmly reminded now. When he was out of the public eye, it was easy to forget. In the middle of it there was no avoiding the fact.

It must be love, this irrational urge to announce to the blonde that Adam Webster was not up for grabs. If not, it was very close to it, Cait decided as the 737 circled to land at San Francisco International. No woman who wasn't just about ready to pull out all the stops could feel as she felt now.

Then again, it was easier and safer to blame the irritation on the stress of the crazy week she had just lived through between her decision to go on tour with Adam and their departure from Seattle together. Taping three segments, and rehearsing and performing three live ones, had been only slightly less than a circus.

Cait smiled to herself, remembering how little effort it had taken to talk Dory into it. Talk? She'd barely gotten past the first word. The zeal with which her matchmaking producer threw herself into the effort was enough to convince anyone the whole project was a Dory Benjamin original.

"True love," she reminded Cait constantly that week, "is nothing you'll ever find *me* standing in the way of."

True love. Was it? Cait glanced over at Adam in the seat next to her. He wore tan wool slacks, a matching sweater and shirt and a charcoal tweed sports coat. Looking at him, Cait couldn't really blame his female admirers. With his dark good looks, he was everything a woman could want. As Cait gazed, the words formed in her mind. *I love you*, Adam. If not easy to voice, it was easier to think with each passing day.

Adam stared, unseeing, into his glass of melting ice. If only persuasion would win out over patience with Cait. Blast her native caution, anyway. But if waiting her out would win her heart, patient he would be.

He felt her glance and turned to meet an expression in her gray eyes that made restraint extremely difficult. The unspoken words were written in the tilt of her up-turned face, the sparkle in her eyes, the vibrant tinge of pink on her cheeks. He clenched the fingers of one hand on his armrest for control. Why, in even their most intimate moments, even when her body was loving his with open abandon, did the words remain locked in her heart?

"Excited, sweet?" he murmured.

She nodded and gave him a sparkly smile as his hand covered hers in her lap. "San Francisco. I can't believe it."

"What's our first sight-seeing stop?"

"Why, the Ghirardelli Chocolate Factory, of course."

"Of course," Adam said with a chuckle. "The chocolate that made Frisco famous. Or was it the other way around?"

"Eat one bite of it and you won't have to ask."

"Can't. Clogs up the old ticker if I don't watch it, remember?" He slid his fingers to the pulse at her wrist. "How's yours, by the way?"

"Fine."

Ignoring the slight stiffening of her wrist, he consulted his watch and counted for a few seconds, then shook his head. "Pretty high for a resting heart rate. When did you last have a medical checkup, sweetheart?"

"Last year. I passed with flying colors."

"But your pulse is—"

He frowned and broke off as Cait pulled away and curled her hand into a tense fist in her lap. Her eyes, alight with a loving glow just the minute before, were now slate-gray blanks. Her cheeks were drained of color.

"Hey, are you feeling all right?" He chucked a finger under her chin to tip her face back so that he could see it.

She didn't reply, just shifted her chin away from his touch and contemplated the pattern on the seat back in front of her.

As slowly and as gently as he could, Adam covered her hand again with his. "Cait, tell me."

"My heart," she said softly, enunciating each word, "is fine. If my pulse is up, it's because I'm excited about the trip. Okay?"

"Sure." He smoothed his knuckles over the back of her hand until it relaxed slightly. "Sure. So am I." After a moment he cleared his throat and leaned closer to add, "I'm also worked up about spending every night for a solid week with you. I've had it with only illicit weekends."

"Adam, hush." Cait darted a swift glance at the man across the aisle. Mercifully he was dozing off the effects of the several complimentary martinis he had imbibed.

"Night after marvelous night, Cait," Adam persevered in an intimate whisper in her ear.

BY THE TIME the taxicab delivered them at the Stanford Court Hotel on Nob Hill, Cait had been wooed into forgetting everything but attaining the privacy of their room as quickly as possible.

Finally there, she puffed out a relieved sigh at how very long the journey from uniformed doorman to the luxury of privacy could be if the guest being accommodated was VIP Adam Webster.

"Does the general manager always welcome you personally to the hotel?" she asked when the solicitous bell captain finally left them alone in their suite. "And the front office manager and the assistant manager, too? Good grief!"

Adam shrugged. "That's fame for you. You learn to live with it. It has its compensations. No cows, for one thing."

Cait crossed the spacious sitting room to inspect the enormous fruit basket on a table. Next to it was a box of Godiva chocolates. "Now *these*—" she held up the box "—are a compensation. Do you always get these, too?"

"That or something similar."

"Yum. I think I can learn to live with this." She slipped the box open, chose a perfectly sculpted chocolate half shell that housed the smoothest of hazelnut praline fillings and bit into it.

Before she could take a second bite, though, Adam moved in on her to pluck the confection from her fingers and return it to the box. His arms slid around her and lifted her into his kiss, and within seconds the sweet lure of hazelnut praline floated away on the warm breeze of a far sweeter temptation.

"Didn't you mention something about sight-seeing this afternoon?" Cait asked in a throaty murmur when she was finally able to surface for air.

"If I did, I forgot to mention *you're* the sight I'd most like to see this afternoon." His fingers splayed out against her back, pressing her forward into his embrace. "Preferably in what you're wearing under what you're wearing."

He slid his palms up and down her back, savoring the firm thrust of her breasts against his chest, the softness of her thighs aligned to the corded muscles of his.

"Adam . . ."

"Hmm?"

"Oh, Adam . . ."

"You're losing ground, I'm afraid."

"Who's trying to keep it?"

"You're a wanton woman, Cait Rafferty."

"You make me that way, Adam Webster."

"My pleasure."

But his greatest pleasure, he knew, would be to hear what she still would not say. He ran a string of kisses from her ear down her throat to the first button of her blouse and tugged at it with his teeth. If only he could free those words from her lips as easily as a button could be released from its hole.

Cait gasped as he swung her up into his arms and carried her to the huge bed in the adjoining bedroom. She marveled, as she often did these days, at the ease with which he did it. So different from Doug, who had always made the maneuver seem more labored than loving.

"Ah, Cait, the things you do to me." He slid his hand down the soft silk of her blouse under her suit jacket and pulled it free of her skirt. "What are you wearing underneath?"

"A teddy."

Another marvel, this fascination of his with what she wore closest to her skin. In addition to paying the rent

and the bills, his advance had allowed her to splurge on
the sensual lingerie he loved and that she loved to wear.

"Silk with lace at the top," he confirmed, eyes closed
as his hand moved up and spread over one breast.
"What color?"

"Lilac, of course."

"Of course." His palm cupped the soft straining
mound higher. First he stroked with his thumb and then
with his fingers.

"You do it just to make me crazy, don't you?"

"I do my best." Cait arched and strained to his touch,
lifted her lips to his and filled his eager mouth with her
tongue.

She tasted of melted chocolate and melting need, a
relentless, rousing flavor that threw Adam headlong
into a fevered impatience he hadn't intended at the start.
Before he could rein in his runaway senses, he had di-
vested Cait of her suit and blouse with a haste out of all
proportion to the leisurely pleasures he'd proposed in
the parlor.

It didn't help that she was undressing him in turn with
equally passionate fervor. Her desire fueled his, pooled
the hot blood in his groin to hard, aching insistence.

"God, hon, I can't slow down."

"Don't, then," Cait whispered. "I want you, too." Her
fingers linked in his hair and guided his mouth down
to where the scalloped edge of the teddy skimmed the
tops of her breasts.

Pert against lilac lace, her nipples rose, inviting the
brush of his lips, the graze of his teeth, the lave of his
tongue in wet circles on the silky material.

Stripped down to just brief jockey shorts, Adam
raised himself up to pull Cait's teddy off and add it to

the garments strewn all around them. Her panty hose followed. Then her fingers were sliding into the elastic at his waist. Warm and searching, they curled around him in a bold caress, then slid his shorts off, leaving him as bare to her touch as she now was to his.

Clasped to each other in a tangle of arms and legs, they fell back into the downy pillows, mouths joined in the deepest of soul kisses.

"We're so good together, sweet. Every time."

"Yes . . . so good . . . O—Ohhh, Adam . . ."

When her thighs opened to his seeking touch, his heart swelled with the pleasure of finding her so hot and ready for the dip and stroke of his fingers. But she always was. Every time. And every time with her was as fresh and new for him as their first time together on the island.

Then she had been almost virginal; his discovery of her body had been her discovery, too. Now, whispering his name in soft pants as he pleasured her, she was all woman, awakened woman, all his if only she would—

"Dear God, I love you," he murmured against her lips. "Love you, do you hear?"

"AdamAdamAdam . . . I—"

Her eyes opened as his fingers moved in a deeper, more intimate caress. Her gaze locked into his, and she saw the waiting in his eyes, felt the pinprick of a tiny tear at each outer corner of hers.

"I . . ."

"What, sweet?"

"I love you, too."

"Oh, God, Cait," he breathed out on a long sigh. "All the way?"

"Over my head."

"Say it again for me."

Her silent but eloquent reply was to gently urge his hips into the cradle of her parted thighs where her body begged to be filled.

"Please, Adam. I need you now."

Cait reached down to guide his pulsing hardness into her but stopped when he smiled, shook his head and twisted slightly away to evade her touch.

"What—"

"Not so fast, sweet. We have all afternoon, remember?"

"But you just said you couldn't—"

"That was before you said those three little words I've been waiting so long to hear. That makes all the difference in the world."

Cait undulated her hips against him and moaned with breathy impatience, "*Please*, Adam."

"Not yet. You took your slow, sweet time getting around to this moment, and now I'm going to enjoy it to the fullest."

She caught her breath and stared at him. Then a rapt, expectant smile parted her lips. "How fully?"

He showed rather than told her, with heavy, drugging kisses meant to steal the breath from her lungs and melt the bones in her limbs. Everywhere he touched her his mouth followed, tasting her smooth flesh from lips to throat to shoulders to breasts to indented navel.

"Ah, Cait, you're beautiful . . . incredible. Lie back, sweet. No, don't touch me."

Even lower he moved, parting her thighs, pressing tiny tongue-kisses on the tender inside of each one until she trembled open to receive the intimate gift he had reserved for this special moment and no other before it.

Cait tensed slightly, but then as Adam's lips and tongue found her, she sighed it all out in a soft, extended ah. It seemed the sound might never end, so great was this pleasure no man had given her until now. So great she could only lace her fingers in his hair breathless minutes later and whisper broken pleas for him to end the exquisite torture.

Her hands left his hair, snaked along his arms to where his hands massaged her breasts. "Adam... Adam, love me."

"Yes, love, yes." He slid up and with a single powerful thrust united his body with hers, filled her as she longed to be filled. They ascended to the final shattering zenith welded together, two bodies, two minds, two hearts coalescing into the singular union of love.

It was only much later, after Adam had carried the basket in from the other room and begun feeding her, one by one, a late, naked lunch of sweet red grapes, that Cait remembered the barely touched chocolates.

Why hadn't he brought them in, too? she suddenly wondered. She opened her mouth to ask. Before she could, though, he popped in another grape and sucked the sweet sphere from her mouth into his. Then they fell laughing together back into the pillows, and she never did get around to asking.

IT WAS JUST AS WELL, Cait decided the next day when she and Adam shared a table in the Ghirardelli Soda Fountain and Chocolate Shop and smiled bedroom smiles at each other. As far as she could tell, the omission was unintended. It hadn't meant a thing. Right now Adam didn't seem to mind at all that she was halfway through a Turkish coffee hot fudge sundae complete with whipped cream, chopped nuts and a two maraschino cherries.

That is, she didn't *think* he minded. It was hard to tell what, exactly, was going on behind the tinted glasses he wore. But he was sipping a cup of French Roast decaf, and his mouth was smiling beneath the reflective lenses of his very effective disguise. That much was certain.

"So what happens tomorrow?" she asked, spoon poised for another scrumptious bite.

"Three radio spots, two TV talk shows and an interview with a feature reporter from the *Chronicle*."

"Then what?"

"A late-afternoon flight to L.A. We have a suite booked at the Bel-Air Hotel."

"First class all the way, huh?"

"Yep, but we won't have time to enjoy it until after the cocktail party with the West Coast publicity people tomorrow night."

"Where do I fit into all this?"

He reached out a hand and clasped one of hers. "Right by my side, whenever possible." His hand tightened. "I didn't want to scare you off by mentioning it before, but a publicity tour of any kind is a grind even at the best of times, Cait. Try to keep that in mind. The week *will* end, I promise."

"Sounds more like a marathon than a book tour."

He shrugged. "In a way it is. That's why we have to stick together and prop each other up over the rough spots."

"In other words, 'Keep on truckin'?"

"Yeah," he said with a chuckle, "and remember those other words of wisdom, 'love conquers all.'" He turned her hand over and traced a seductive design over the surface of her palm.

"All I can remember right now is that wise old saying, opposites attract," Cait murmured with a catch in her voice. He was as addicting as the rarest chocolate, she thought, and she craved him like a rush of pure sugar in the bloodstream.

"Hmm. Know what *I* say, sweet?"

"What?"

"Let's go back to the hotel and attract for an hour or two before we hit Chinatown."

Cait glanced down at her half-finished sundae, his half-drunk coffee and then up at the provocative half smile on Adam's lips.

Was there any contest? Before she could say Ghirardelli, the check was paid and she and Adam were out the door.

9

AS BEFITTED A WOMAN in the throes of true love, Cait was deliriously happy. Delirious enough to push that abandoned hot fudge sundae back to the Siberian wastes of her mind and leave it in cold storage for the remainder of the weekend.

It was simply a coincidence, she told herself, like the similarly abandoned Godiva chocolates. And if Adam hustled her into walking a few more uphill blocks than she suspected were really necessary for a tour of Chinatown, what of it? The same went for the Szechuan red snapper and steamed vegetable dinner they ended up eating at a charming hole-in-the wall Szechuan restaurant.

So what if the meal was low-fat, low-cholesterol, low-cal and not quite the tortellini in prosciutto-cream sauce she'd envisioned dining on in North Beach? Adam was, after all, a man who couldn't exactly afford to eat his way into another bypass.

Besides, the six fortune cookies she splurged on for dessert were excellent. Sweet and extraordinarily crispy, they contained six most fortuitous fortunes, too. Between Adam and great good fortune, what more, really, could she want?

Complete peace of mind, a tiny interior voice replied. *An end to the nagging possibility that the walks,*

*the impromptu swims, the interrupted snacks are more
frequent than coincidence alone can explain away.*

Telling herself she was just gun-shy, Cait put a mental gag on that little voice and concentrated on Adam. Now there was a thing easily done. Now that she had finally opened the doors of her heart to him, he was as easy to love as chocolate or anything else, for that matter, had ever been. More so.

She was besotted.

SO WAS EVERY ADAM WEBSTER fan in San Francisco and L.A., she discovered as the week got under way. So was every TV talk-show host and radio interviewer and bookseller in both cities. So were the inevitable groupies. Though Cait had known in advance this would be the case, she still hadn't been prepared for the sensation of being the excess baggage she felt like by sunset on Monday evening at the Bel-Air Hotel.

What could prepare one plump, reasonably attractive female, on the arm of the man she loved, to stand by in smiling silence while a second female, the gorgeous star of several sexy movies, put a finger on his lapel and cooed, "You're really and truly Adam Webster? Do you mind if I touch you, darling?"

What preparation could there possibly be to counteract it? None, Cait decided as she sipped a brandy alexander at the cocktail party that night. Nothing could prepare a woman in love for the likes of that. She stifled a sigh and bent a polite ear to what Adam's stout, balding West-Coast publicity agent was saying about his famous client.

Across the reception room, Adam stood surrounded by a knot of male and female admirers so tight

Cait had given up any hope of regaining the place at his side she had immediately lost. Occupying that spot now and holding it was the sexy film star, Marissa Maine.

It hadn't escaped Cait that the blond beauty's slim yet fabulous figure took up only half the space at Adam's side that hers had. In fact, Cait couldn't help further noticing, not one of the hundred or so party guests assembled carried what anyone could even remotely term an excess pound of flesh. Except for her and Adam's agent, that was.

"Great guy, there," the fast-talking agent was declaring with a stab of his stubby cigar in Adam's direction. "Getting famous and scoring the big buckolas can do screwy things to some people. Most of 'em, in fact. But not him. I mean, how many people do you know who made the cover of *People* three times in one year and stayed human?"

Cait cast a wry eye at the blond bombshell and replied, "How about her for starters? She's on the covers of at least four different magazines this month alone, judging by the supermarket racks."

"Five," the agent corrected, "but she doesn't count."

"Why not?"

He took a puff of his cigar and blew the thick smoke out with obvious relish before answering, "Because a woman who looks like Marissa Maine isn't human. Any woman who looks like that is divine."

With a capital *D*, Cait added silently before she excused herself and beat a hasty retreat out of the reception room and down the hall. Stealing a moment alone out of the tight tour schedule or away from the crowd was something Cait had quickly learned could be done in a pinch only in the nearest ladies' room.

Luckily both the mirrored lounge and its adjoining rest room were empty. With a sigh of relief Cait locked herself into a stall and sat down on the closed toilet-seat lid to collect her thoughts.

When Adam had said it would be grueling, she hadn't fully understood what he meant. Two days later she did. Already she was feeling fatigued by the nonstop schedule. Fatigue, however, wasn't the worst part. The worst part was the obvious. Adam had evidently forgotten to mention anything about *that*.

Then again, why would he? Certainly there could be nothing grueling to him or any other red-blooded male about having Marissa Maine hanging on his arm and his every word. The strain was in being the bystander who watched. It lay in being the one who got trampled underfoot in his admiring public's rush for autographs at airports, hotels, restaurants, you name it.

She sighed, suddenly reminded of her wallflower days in high school.

"You don't have to go if you don't want to, dear," her mother had said each time a school dance was announced.

"You don't understand, Mom," Cait remembered insisting grimly, "I *have* to go."

Few things were worse than sitting out four years of dances on the sidelines with only Georgina Schuyler, six feet tall and known as The Skyscraper, for company. Of those few, not going to the dance at all was worse. Cait knew it. Georgina knew it. Being treated like social poison by the boys was one thing; admitting the creeps were right by staying home was another.

Now, years later, she sat wishing she had stayed in Seattle and never come on the tour with Adam. At the realization that the wish was a throwback to days long gone, she squared her shoulders a little. Good Lord, why was she thinking of that now? That was all behind her now, wasn't it?

Of course it was. Except that she was definitely feeling like overly flowery wallpaper again. But that was ridiculous, considering she was no longer the Miss Piggy of an adolescent she had been, no longer social poison. And neither was The Skyscraper, she hastened to remind herself. The last she had heard, Georgina was a highly paid New York model.

So there. Feeling slightly foolish, she stood and smoothed the sleeveless raw silk tunic she wore over matching black evening pants. When she'd bought the size fourteen outfit three weeks ago in Seattle, it had fit perfectly. Putting it on in the hotel room an hour earlier, though, she noticed the pants felt looser at the waist and hips. But she'd been too rushed to think about it any further.

Now she ran an exploratory forefinger between the pants' waistband and her own waist. There was almost an inch to spare. Cait frowned. She never lost weight, or gained it, in fact. Ever since her recovery from Doug, her weight had remained stable and predictable, year in and year out, no matter what.

She couldn't possibly have lost. Or... or could she? Slowly she sat back down. The walks. The swims. The grapes instead of Godivas. The—

She tensed as lilting laughter sounded from the outer lounge. Then she heard the inner door swing open to admit what sounded like two women.

"Have you ever in your life seen eyes like that?" inquired one female voice that Cait had no trouble identifying as the predatory variety.

"No, and neither has Marissa, from the looks of it," the other replied. "Is she here with him, do you think?"

"No, he came in with someone else, but it's crystal clear Marissa's dying to trade places. I can't believe the way she's monopolizing him."

"I can. If I had the chance, I'd do the same. Did you hear her tell him she practically sleeps with his books under her pillow?"

"Yeah. She beat me to it. So do I."

"I can't say I go quite that far, but I *can* say in all honesty I'd follow him to the ends of the earth if he crooked his finger at me. What would I be today if it hadn't been for him?"

"How about fat and divorced and depressed?"

"You should talk. Running saved you from the same fate, too."

"You notice I didn't bring hubby, though."

"I noticed. You sneak. I wish I had thought of that. I haven't been able to get a really good ogle in all night."

They both giggled while Cait wrestled with the tumult of conflicting emotions in her breast. *He's all mine,* she longed to burst out of her stall and say. *He loves me and I love him, and as for all you Marissa Maines and Samanthas out there, eyes and hands off! And he isn't responsible for saving your marriages and thinning you down and getting you happy, either. His book did the opposite for me four years ago, for heaven's sake.*

The giggles subsided, toilets flushed, and then Cait heard the noisy splash of the two washing their hands.

"So who's the lucky someone he's here with, anyway? Not Danielle, I hope, like the last time."

Cait's heart sank. Danielle who? Last time when?

"No. Dani's ancient history. I've never seen this one before now, but I can tell you one thing for sure."

"What?"

"She's nowhere near the same league as Danielle or Marissa. She doesn't run."

"You're kidding."

"I kid you not. Remember what we looked like before we both read *Runner's High* and worked up to five miles a day? That's her."

"You can't be serious."

"See for yourself. I'll point her out to you when we get back. She's wearing black, loose and blousy, and you know what that means."

"I'll say. Cellulite City underneath."

"Exactly."

"What's he doing with someone like that?"

"You tell me and we'll both know."

The inner door opened and closed as they left. Cait sat quite still in the sudden silence with a lump of tears jamming her throat. Not only was she feeling more the wallflower than she had a moment before, but there it was, the same question she had asked Dory weeks before. The same one she had asked herself a million times since meeting Adam. Why Cait when there were zillions waiting in the wings who had moved out of, or maybe never even inhabited, Cellulite City?

Because he fell in love with you, just like he said, she told herself and knew that much was true. Adam was an honest man. Heartened by that indisputable fact, she forced the tears back an inch. He wouldn't have said it if he hadn't meant it. Still, it wasn't proof that his love was unconditional.

If it hadn't been for Doug, she wouldn't now have reason to wonder what expectations might be wedded to Adam's love. Because of Doug, though, she had reason enough. The fact remained that altering her physical proportions to Doug's altered tastes had become a big item on his love agenda. Cait had never doubted that if she had only kept up the running, kept off the weight and revised her daily menu to imitate Doug's, he would never have looked at another woman.

But she hadn't. And he had.

But like Danielle, wasn't that ancient history, too? Holding the tears back, she shook off the memories and rose to her feet. That was all behind her now. She was her own woman now, not the malleable putty she had been in Doug's demanding hands. She didn't have to stand in front of mirrors these days and agonize over every little ripple and bulge as if each was a species of social disease.

Staunchly ignoring every mirror, she walked out of the lounge and back to the party. Yet she couldn't quite shake the beastly question, "What's he doing with someone like that?"

THE NEXT MORNING Cait gazed up into the deep green of Adam's eyes and wondered what she could have possibly been thinking of the night before. In the magical aftermath of morning lovemaking, the answer to the question seemed potently clear: He was doing what came naturally.

"Mmm," Adam whispered. "I'm going to take you along on all my book tours from now on. I'll never need a wake-up call again."

Cait shifted to her side and snuggled her back into the warm haven of his chest. "And *I'll* never need to pack a travel alarm if you keep this up, Adam."

"Me? I'm not the one who can't stay on my side of the bed." He gathered her close and cupped a caressing hand to the curve of one of her breasts.

"You steal the covers," Cait remonstrated with a dreamy smile. "I get chilly."

"I'll order twin beds for us from now on."

"Do it and die."

Adam chuckled and draped a leg possessively over her. "Wild horses couldn't make me. How could I rise and shine in twin beds?"

"Ozzie and Harriet managed somehow."

"I like the way *we* manage. I love you, sweet."

"I love you, too."

As answers to questions went, how could she ask for more? The brandy alexander, she decided with an audible sigh, must have gone to her head the night before. Cait covered his hand at her breast with hers. Adam was with her for all the obvious reasons. Even now he was murmuring words of love over and over, soft and warm into her ear. Even now his arms clasped her and held her to him as if he would never let go.

It took the ring of the phone announcing their wake-up call to force his embrace away. Cait stretched from fingertip to toe, wishing the feeling of total completion would never wane, wishing she could have him to herself all day.

Adam thanked the operator, hung up and turned back to Cait. Planting a peck of a kiss on the tip of her nose, he murmured, "How about a swim? We have plenty of time now that we've—" He stopped and grinned.

"Swim?" Cait repeated on the long exhalation of a languorous yawn.

Adam nodded. "What better way to start the day in sunny California?"

Cait lifted her head from the pillows and watched as he got out of bed to fling open the curtains on the kind of golden day that seldom occurred in Seattle. A morning swim, she thought with a prick of foreboding.

"I didn't bring a suit."

Wearing the suit he was born in, he turned from the window. "How about a walk, then?"

"What about breakfast?"

Adam bounded over to the phone. "Room service coming right up, Madam." He dialed and ordered, "Two oatmeals with skim milk, a fresh fruit platter, whole-wheat toast and decaffeinated coffee." He paused and grinned at Cait. "Yes. We'd like that in an hour. Right. Thank you."

He hung up with a flourish and leaned over the bed to kiss Cait's nose again. "Rise and shine, sleepyhead. I'll be out of the shower in a sec."

Slowly Cait lowered her head back into the pillows. Then she curled her body into a ball and burrowed her head under them. The pillows muffled the happy sound of Adam singing off-key in the shower while a crowd of unhappy thoughts chorused in perfect harmony in her head.

As assumptions went, the ones Adam had so blithely made a moment ago were in a class by themselves. A walk was one thing. Though loath to admit it, she had actually begun to enjoy putting one foot in front of the other during these increasingly frequent strolls with Adam. But oatmeal for breakfast—with skim milk, yet—*without* consulting her was something else entirely.

Cait curled tighter into her fetal position as every doubt, fear and qualm she had ever had rose like a tidal wave and washed away the sweet languor of loving Adam. Up with the fears and qualms rose that beast of a question from the night before. She bunched the pillows tight over her ears. Skim milk. *Oat*meal. Yech. It was enough to make a body—especially a body like Cait the Cook's—do something rash.

Something like heading that oatmeal off at the pass, to be precise. With a grimace she flung off the pillows, uncoiled her legs and arms and reached for the phone. After replacing her half of Adam's earlier room service order with her own selection, she added that she and Adam had changed their minds and would like breakfast brought in ASAP.

With that done, she settled back against the headboard of the bed and pondered the beast again. Ferocious monster of a thing. If only the question could be answered once and for all without a shred of a doubt.

In the bathroom Adam lowered his rich baritone to a hum as he turned the shower off and stepped out to towel down. He couldn't remember ever singing in the shower after the first of his numerous tours. He'd never had much reason after that baptism of fire. Now, with

Cait, he did. *That's what true love can do for you. Way to go, Webster.*

In the first flush of his success, though, he'd been dazzled almost blind by everything. Including the women, like Marissa Maine. But only at first. He could only shake his head now at the memory as he lathered up to shave. Fresh off the farm, he had taken awhile to realize what most of them really wanted—and it wasn't the private Adam Webster. Most wanted only to bask in his superstar spotlight, to savor a vicarious taste of his fame.

Not Cait. The day before, when things got rolling in San Francisco, he had taken note of her slightly stunned expression. Last night, he recalled gratefully, she had still worn it. It was a good thing. Though the attendant publicity was a necessary evil, there was nothing natural or normal about being a celebrity author on a book tour. For no reason he had ever been able to pinpoint, the Marissa Maines were part and parcel of it. He was glad Cait appreciated the unreality of it enough to remain dazed.

He plugged in his pistol hair dryer and turned it on full blast. Thank God he had moved from Manhattan to Seattle and found Cait. She alone, in this media blitz of a tour, was real to him. So real it was hard now to imagine a day without her. Or a month, or a year, or a life without Cait in it.

Or a bed, to be sure. He grinned into the mirror. Even now, after an hour of glorying in what had to be one of the best awakenings of his entire life, his body stirred with wanting Cait again. Oh, she was real, all right—and the best part of his life, bar none. Best of all, she loved the real him.

He was still grinning when he walked out of the bathroom with a towel wrapped around his hips and saw Cait bite into the Mr. Goodbar.

10

"HEY, WHAT GOES THERE?" Adam's satisfied grin faltered slightly as he eyed the candy bar at Cait's lips.

"Just a snack before breakfast," Cait replied around a mouthful of chocolate and peanuts. With her shoulders propped against the padded headboard of the bed, she flicked a nonexistent crumb off the long white terry robe she now wore. "Want a bite?" she invited, proffering the chocolate bar in Adam's direction.

"Uh, no, thanks."

Cait saw his smile contract into an expression of utter disbelief when he saw the three crumpled wrappers in her lap.

"That's...quite a...a snack," he got out after blinking several times at them.

"I get carried away sometimes." Cait brightened her fake smile even further and took another bite. She thought of the two unwrapped, uneaten bars stashed in her purse on the floor next to the bed. Maybe she shouldn't have gone quite so far as to make it seem that she was deep into her third candy bar. If the look on Adam's face was anything to go by, two would have been plenty.

"But, Cait—three before breakfast?" he inquired, his voice rising in unmistakable incredulity.

Cait shrugged and glanced down at the wrappers. "Three different kinds—I hate to play favorites. And like Mount Everest, they were just *there*. Once I got started, it was too good to stop."

"Maybe it'd be easier if you just carried one around with you," Adam said after a moment of silence. He came over to sit on the edge of the bed opposite Cait. "How can you do that on an empty stomach?"

Taking note of the definite grimace that accompanied his query, she replied, "Easy."

Adam blinked again. "All that sugar and fat? You must know what too much of that stuff can do to you?"

"Of course I do. Without it I wouldn't be the author of *Chocolate à la Carte* or the resident cook on *Northwest Live*. For *me*, it's done wonders." She popped the last bite into her mouth and girded for battle. She could already see, from the dark frown creasing Adam's brow, that battle it would be.

"You could still exercise some restraint, sweet. Good God, three in one morning."

"Beats oatmeal and dry toast, if you ask me."

"Those," he said, pointing at the wrappers, "will never beat out real food in the breakfast sweepstakes."

"'Real food' meaning what *you* ordered for *me* from room service, I take it?"

"Cait, we have a long day ahead of us. Three candy bars isn't going to see you through to lunch, believe me. You need—"

"A brisk walk and a foursquare breakfast to start the day right," she interjected with a knowing scowl. "Save the sermon for the talk shows. I already know you think I eat too much junk food for my own good. You just haven't had the nerve to say it. That's it, isn't it?"

He stood, his hands clenched at his sides. "In a nut-shell," he admitted. "But it doesn't take an expert like me to know you should cut back on the sweets."

Cait balled up the last candy wrapper in her hand and dropped it with a flourish into the pile in her lap. "I assume that's why you've been interfering with my intake recently. You have, haven't you?"

"So what if I have?" His mouth hardened. "Diverting your attention to greater pleasures is no mortal sin. And you can't say you weren't readily diverted, sweet. Or just as readily pleasured."

Crumpled wrappers went flying as Adam's ready admission spurred Cait off the bed. Raking the agitated fingers of one hand through the auburn tangle of her curls, she faced him across the king-size expanse of rumpled sheets.

"What else have you been thinking that you haven't had the nerve to say out loud, Adam?" she inquired.

"Right now I can't help wondering how you can eat that garbage right after making love to me like I was the last man on earth."

Garbage. Cait met Adam's fiery gaze with one of her own. Now there was an epithet guaranteed to rouse the ire of any self-respecting chocoholic. Garbage, wasn't it? Good thing the walls of the swank Bel-Air were nice and thick. A few notes higher and they would both be shouting.

"Next you'll be telling me I should lose the extra twenty-five pounds *you* just made love to as if they were the last pounds on earth," she shot back. "Or were you counting on the swims and walks and bike rides to do the trick?"

Tall, dark and unutterably attractive even with the green flare of anger in his eyes, Adam stood girded by only the white towel around his lean hips. "Every extra pound is a strain on a heart that isn't exercised regularly," he asserted. "If you lose a pound or two in the process, those are the breaks."

"So!" Cait dug her heels into the plush carpet. "I wasn't imagining things after all. That bike ride, the walks to the lake, all of it was deliberate. As casual as could be, but deliberate just the same."

Silence crackled like live electricity before he said, "Only because I love you, Cait. Your health is as much my concern as mine is. I—"

A knock at the door stopped him. He threw a quizzical glance in the direction of the sound and then back at Cait.

"Breakfast," she said tersely.

"Now? What—"

"Coming," she called out. Skirting Adam and the bed, she went into the parlor and let the waiter in with their breakfast cart.

"Thanks, we'll serve ourselves," she told the young man after she signed the check.

He left and she wheeled the cart into the bedroom, where Adam still stood with his hands on his hips. "You were saying?" she prompted.

"What about the walk?"

"I've changed my mind."

Adam didn't say a word as Cait poured herself a cup of coffee and carried it over to the nightstand on her side of the bed. He remained silent, watching, as she sat back against the headboard again with her arms folded in front of her.

"Cait..."

"What?"

"I think we *need* a walk. To blow the steam off."

"If we do, your oatmeal will get cold and so will my waffle."

"Your what?"

"My chocolate-chip Belgian waffle with whipped cream and—"

Adam held up a restraining hand. "Don't tell me. Chocolate syrup, right?"

"Any objections?"

"Would it make a difference?"

"My health is my own concern."

"Not much of one, from what I can see." Adam threw the words over his shoulder as he crossed to the cart and lifted the lid from his oatmeal.

"According to my doctor, I'm in perfect health. Whatever awful things fat and sugar do to some people's arteries, they don't do to mine."

"Easy to say when it hasn't caught up with you yet." He poured milk on his cereal, stabbed a spoon into it and pulled the cart over to his side of the bed, where he settled against the headboard next to Cait. "You aren't really going to eat that, are you?" he asked, eyeing the domed cover on the plate next to his oatmeal.

"I certainly am." She stared straight ahead and tightened her arms across her chest. Out of the corner of her eye, though, she saw Adam's lips purse and then harden again.

"Okay," he said after a moment. He uncovered her plate and handed it over to her with a fork and a napkin. "Eat it. What difference does it make that I love you enough to care what happens to you?"

"What's wrong with loving me just as I am?" She stared down, unseeing, at the contents of her plate. "Just tell me that."

"Cait, would I have spent the time and effort to help you change at your own pace if I didn't love you so much it hurts? Good God, woman, it's not as if you're any worse off. And you can't say we didn't have fun together biking and walking and swimming—the sort of fun two people could have together for a lifetime, if they wanted."

Cait caught her breath and swallowed hard on the unmistakable softening she heard in his tone. Those *had* been wonderful fun- and laughter-filled times. Better than any she had ever known with another human being. But she couldn't afford to fall prey to his colossal charm this time, she warned herself. She couldn't waver in the face of this. After all, hadn't every vague suspicion she had earlier dismissed as coincidence just been proven true? Give him an inch now, and he'd take a mile in a minute.

Yes, indeed. Adam's hidden agenda was hidden no more. The only thing left to do was to stick to her own agenda through thick and thin.

She swirled a forkful of waffle in the thick, dark syrup poured over it and lifted it, dripping, to her mouth. But there was little joy to be had in forcing it past the angry lump of tears that had begun to form in her throat. In her stomach the candy bar she had eaten felt like a huge stone.

She set her fork down. Damn. He had some nerve defending himself by saying she wasn't any worse off. That it was true was beside the point. Hadn't he ever heard of live and let live?

Adam glanced over at her and raised an eyebrow. "How's the waffle?"

"Perfect."

"Oh? Is that why you're wolfing it down like there's no tomorrow?"

"It wins hands down over the breakfast conversation at the moment."

"You started it with those appetizers of yours, Cait."

Cait slapped her plate down on the bed with a dull thud. "I have a perfect right to eat whatever I want, whenever I want without a running commentary from you."

"Speaking of running, excuse me while I go for a long one." With that Adam slammed his oatmeal bowl down into the mound of whipped cream on Cait's waffle.

Acting on impulse, Cait reached down to the side of the bed for her purse. How fortunate that she had pushed the issue, she told herself. Now she knew, without a doubt. Fuming, she dug past the two candy bars in her purse to the very bottom.

In the same time it took Adam to pull a pair of red running shorts out of his suitcase, Cait put a cigarette to her lips and struck a match.

Adam whipped around at the hiss of the flame. "You . . . you smoke, too?" he said after a stunned moment.

"Brilliant deduction." Cait held the lit match to the cigarette and took a long drag before extinguishing the flame with a shaky puff. Blowing the smoke out through her nostrils, she dropped the spent matchstick in Adam's oatmeal.

Stock-still, he stared at her. "Why didn't you tell me you were a smoker?"

"Why didn't you tell *me* you thought I needed re-forming?"

"Listen, Cait, all I'm guilty of is giving you a pain-less introduction to a healthier, more active life. I never once preached or proselytized or forced you to do anything you weren't willing to do."

Unable to refute him, Cait blew a smoke ring into the air and tried to keep her eyes fixed on that small diversion rather than the major diversion of Adam throwing off his towel and pulling on his running shorts. During that brief moment of total nudity in between the throwing and the pulling, she knew that he knew she hadn't succeeded at her task.

"How long has this been going on?" he asked as he fished a pair of socks from a duffel bag.

"Since right after I got dis-engaged."

"So chocolate isn't your only vice."

"Of course it it. This is just an indulgence."

"Great. So where have you been 'indulging' for the past month? In the closet?"

"No. In the privacy of my own room in my own bed after my morning alarm goes off."

He sat down at the foot of the bed and pulled on a sock with a grunt. "Why haven't you smoked around me before?"

"Does it matter that I do?"

"Does it matter?" he parroted as if she'd just replied in a foreign language.

"Well?" she prodded, lifting the cigarette to her lips again for another deep drag.

"What do *you* think?" he snapped in reply.

But Cait couldn't answer. Instead of proceeding straight to her lungs, the smoke she had inhaled took a side path straight down the wrong windpipe. Her shoulders shook as a coughing fit overtook her. Through the watery blur of tears evoked by the smoky seizure, she saw Adam's eyebrows knot into a tight frown as he came around the bed to her.

"Serves you right to choke on your own smoke," he contended darkly. "Here, lean over for a sec."

He dropped down on the edge of the mattress, bent her forward and whacked her with the flat of his hand between her shoulder blades until she had neither smoke nor air left in her lungs.

"Enough, enough." Cait wheezed and choked and tried to pull away. But Adam's hold was so strong she only succeeded in singeing a spot on the sheet with the lit cigarette in her flailing hand.

Thwack! Thwack! Muttering ripe imprecations under his breath, Adam redoubled his already successful efforts to resuscitate her.

"Stop! Let me up!" Cait finally sucked in enough air to yelp out.

"Are you okay?"

Though the inquiry was one of concern, it was spoken in a tone so harsh Cait was taken aback for a moment. She had never heard him use that tone. Nor had she ever seen his eyes turn such a dark and storm-tossed green. As for the tiny muscle that flexed in his jaw, she almost quailed at the sight of it. Tension was coiled in it like a bullwhip, ready to lash out with only the slightest provocation.

"I'm fine . . . really."

"You don't *look* fine. Your face is all red, and your hair's standing on— Here, give me that thing."

With a swipe of his hand he plucked the cigarette from between her trembling fingers. Another sweeping movement of his tanned, muscled arm stubbed it out in her waffle.

"What's going on here, Cait?" He turned back to her, his expression as grouchy as his voice was gruff.

"Nothing to get so bent out of shape about," she bristled in return. "The smoke just ends up going down the wrong hatch every once in a while."

"Too bad it doesn't go down wrong every time," he muttered. "Why didn't you tell me you were a smoker?"

"Because I'm not—exactly."

He cast an incredulous glance at the chocolate-sodden cigarette in the bowl. "Give me a break. You sure as hell looked like the real thing to me."

"The real thing doesn't smoke just one a day in the morning."

"One? Why in hell do you even bother with the damned things?"

"Why don't *you* go on that long run and stop asking ridiculous questions?"

He stared hard into her eyes. "Maybe I shouldn't go anywhere until we get a few things straightened out here."

"We've already gotten a few things straightened out here, Adam," Cait retorted. "I'm a chocoholic, a sofa spud and a sometime smoker. You're a closet reformer who can't live with someone like me and let live."

"The fact remains, Cait, all that sugar and fat and smoke and no exercise at all isn't good for you."

"The fact also remains that if I wanted your unsolicited advice, I'd have bought your books a long time ago and practiced what you preach. Furthermore—"

But she never got further because the phone on the opposite side of the bed rang. Adam got up and yanked it to his ear with an impatient scowl.

"Yes. Yes. Just a sec." He looked at Cait and covered the receiver with his cupped palm. "Your editor. Ainsley."

Cait stood. "I'll take it in the sitting room."

"I'll be back in forty-five minutes." Adam's voice was harsh. "Just remember, we've got to be out of here and on our way to that morning talk show by nine. We can discuss this later."

"Correction," Cait retorted as she swept to the bedroom door with exaggerated dignity. "*You're* the one who has to be there on time. It's not *my* famous lips the groupies out there want to hear the gospel according to aerobics drip from today."

"And just what do you plan to do here all alone?"

"Smoke one whole cigarette in peace, that's what."

"Fine. Go ahead." He tightened his palm over the receiver. "Smoke it. Order another waffle. Better yet, smoke the whole damned pack and order *two* waffles. Do it up big."

"Maybe I will." She glared at him in sudden decision. "I might even do it on the next plane back to Seattle."

"You'd leave in the middle of everything?"

"The sooner the better!"

"So much for caution, in other words!"

"Yes. I finally dove in headfirst, and now I'm diving out the same way!"

"Go home, then. Maybe you'll get lucky there and find a real peach of a guy who doesn't mind kissing a woman who tastes like an ashtray in the morning." He glanced at the receiver he still held. "Are you going to talk to this clown? Or should I tell him you're too busy packing enough cigarettes and candy bars for the trip home to talk right now?"

"Jeremy Ainsley is not the clown here." Cait threw Adam a withering glare and slammed the bedroom door shut behind her. Stalking to the phone, she took three deep breaths that did nothing to calm the trembling in her body and picked up the receiver.

"Hi, Jer." She heard the overly loud click of Adam hanging up the extension. "What's up?"

"From the sound of things, it's your dander. Did I interrupt something I shouldn't have?"

"No, not a thing. I was just, er, making arrangements to fly home today."

"Home? But when you last called, you said you'd be on tour with Webster all week. What gives?"

Cait sighed. "It's a long story. The sad short end of it is I'm heading home as soon as I can get a flight out. What can I do for you?"

"Me? Uh, oh, yeah. I'm calling to set up a— Hey, now, there's an idea. In fact—"

He broke off and Cait heard the shuffling of papers over the faint static on the line. Through the closed bedroom door she could hear the much louder than necessary banging of drawers as Adam got dressed.

"Set up a what, Jer?"

"Um, it'll be cutting things awfully close, of course, but it's better than waiting until after Thanksgiving. Yeah, lots better. Listen, how would you like to fly to New York instead of Seattle today?"

"Me?"

"I'll pick you up at the airport if you'll come."

"Come for what?"

"Would you believe a book tour?"

UNBELIEVABLE. There was no other word for it, Cait thought the next morning as she stood next to the former Miss America who hosted *Bite the Big Apple* and watched the perky brunette hold *Chocolate à la Carte* up to the TV camera trained on it.

Forty floors below early-November snow frosted the busy sidewalks of midtown Manhattan. Inside the studio, though, it was as warm and bright under the massed lights as winter had been in the blossom-lush garden of the Bel-Air Hotel just the day before.

"This is *it*!" Tess Byers told the studio audience and millions of New Yorkers watching out in television land that very second. "Chocolate cookbooks come and go, as every chocophile knows, but *this* one tops the list of what *Bite* thinks a chocolate cookbook should be. Please join me in giving a Big Apple welcome to the author you're sure to be hearing a lot more about after today's show—Cait Rafferty."

The fifty or so people in the studio audience greeted her with enthusiastic applause. Among them was Jeremy, a bespectacled beanpole of a man in baggy tweeds, accompanied by his wife and two adult daughters. Catching Cait's eye, he gave her a thumbs-up sign.

Cait smiled back, hoping the minimicrophone clamped to the bib of her royal-blue apron couldn't pick up the sound of her heart breaking. It was bad enough that under the heavy stage makeup her eyelids were still puffy from crying her heart out half the night.

Combined with her first taste of jet lag, it was all enough to make her wish she had never written the book, never opted to do *Northwest Live* and never been unlucky enough to so much as meet Adam Webster.

"Cait," Tess said, "your publisher says *Chocolate à la Carte* is gaining bigger advance sales than any other speciality cookbook being published this season. How does it feel to know your first book is a winner?"

"I'm thrilled, Tess," Cait lied through smiling, petroleum-jellied lips. "Just thrilled."

Any other time it would have been the truth. Any other time she would have been prostrate with excitement. Now the only word for what she felt was miserable, so miserable she couldn't even freeze with stage fright. She couldn't show it, though, she reminded herself. As Dory always said, "Give 'em your best, or get out of the business."

That was the thing to remember. She owed nothing less than her best to her publisher, her public and especially Jeremy, who had lobbied hard with the publicity department to promote the book with an East Coast minitour. It was he who had scrambled to rearrange the schedule overnight after learning Cait was free for the rest of the week.

"Well," said Tess, "we're thrilled to have you on the show. Which one of all the marvelous goodies in the book are you going to cook today?"

"Chocolate Pecan Pie. You know, Thanksgiving is just around the corner, and if you're like me, every few years you say to yourself, 'This time I'm going to give the Great Pumpkin a break and bake something different.' Well, this pie is different, easy and has a splash of dark rum in it to make it truly something to give thanks for."

With a determined grin directed at Jeremy, she launched into the demonstration. For that sweetheart of a man and his nice family she would break a leg, no matter how much it hurt.

It ended up hurting more than anything ever had. Two more talk-show appearances and an afternoon of bookstore autographs later, Cait had given it her best. As acts went, she knew hers could have won an Oscar or a Tony for light comedy. She had even managed to look blasé when three men seeking her autograph on separate occasions had asked her outright to marry them.

What really hurt was remembering Adam dealing with the same proposals from strange women. She knew now he hadn't deserved the jealousy she'd secretly felt. For anyone in the public eye it seemed to come with the territory.

After an early dinner at "21" with Jeremy, she let herself into her St. Regis Hotel room and flopped down fully clothed and overcoated on the bed. Was it really only Wednesday? It felt like the end of the world.

Tomorrow Pittsburgh and Baltimore awaited with the same routine to be repeated. Friday it was on to Boston and Philadelphia for the same thing. On Saturday she would return to New York for a live demonstration in the morning at Bloomingdale's—if she was still alive.

Fat chance. She hadn't felt alive since she left L.A. Cait stared at the ceiling as tears welled up and rolled from the outer corners of her eyes down her temples and into her hair. Last night had been a living hell. She'd missed Adam awfully then and missed him even more now. One night of pure misery and three more like it to go.

Now she knew why Adam hadn't been gunning his engine to get on the road. It seemed aeons ago that she had burst at the seams with excitement when he announced his tour. Aeons ago that he had burst at the seams when she said she'd go with him. Now she knew firsthand what he meant about lying alone in a bed in a lonely hotel room in the middle of a strange city.

Adam. Oh, Adam. She flung a forearm over her eyes to block out the thought of the bed and the man she had left behind at the Bel-Air Hotel. It did no good. She could still see the love-rumpled sheets. She could still see him stalking out of the suite ten minutes late for the show he was appearing on.

Nothing she did could block any of it out. She could still hear the resounding slam of the door, still hear his last terse words: "Say hi to the M&M&Ms for me."

Where was he now? She went through a mental checklist of his itinerary. He'd done Dallas today and was landing at the Kansas City airport right now. Tomorrow night he'd arrive here in New York, but by then she'd have already done Philadelphia and be on a late-evening flight to Boston. By the time he hit Boston for Friday-afternoon appearances, she would be finished with her morning schedule there and be landing in Pittsburgh for the afternoon. Never the twain would meet.

Even if she *wanted* the twain to meet, it would not happen, not until Seattle. But she couldn't stand to think of home and the cats and Dory's face falling when she found out it was not true love at all.

She sat up and dabbed at her eyes with her coat sleeve. This had to stop. She couldn't schlepp around the country on her first book tour with pink marshmallows for eyes. It had to stop, but how to stop it?

She glanced morosely around the silent room and paused at the bouquet of fresh flowers and the pound of chocolates on the mahogany secretary in the far corner of the room. Jeremy had ordered them placed there for her arrival, but she had barely noticed them until now. Now her eyes brightened through the mist of tears. There, within reach, was the one thing that had never failed her.

She stood and shucked off her coat. Doug had failed her. Adam had failed her. Her heart had failed her. But chocolate? Not once. Here was comfort food of the highest order. Brightening with each step, she crossed to the secretary and inspected the box. They were the best, imported from Belgium. Heaven.

Sniffing away her tears more easily now, Cait slipped the lid off and gasped. Better than heaven, here was a whole pound of her favorite pieces, each composed of a layer of marzipan, another of coffee cream, a walnut layer and last a coating of dark chocolate.

She had just lifted the first one to within an inch of her parted lips when the phone rang. At the sound she lowered the candy an inch and snapped her mouth shut.

Ring. This was uncanny. Only one person could possibly be calling at this precise moment. *Ring.* Though it defied logic, she knew with the conviction of instinct who it was. *Ring.* The caller was not Mom or Dad or Dory or Jeremy or anyone else.

Ring. It could only be the only someone who had separated her from more bites of sheer heaven than she wanted to remember. *Ring.* Belgian chocolates or Adam Webster. Which would it be?

DRESSED FOR AN EVENING RUN in sweatshirt, sweat-pants and a new pair of Adidas, Adam stopped on his way out the door of his Kansas City hotel suite when the phone rang. Cait, was his first thought. *Ring.* He stepped back inside and stared at the phone.

Ring. There was only one person who had ever caused him to willingly put off a five-mile run. *Ring.* It had to be her. He'd already talked with his mother, his agent, his publicist and Masuo in the previous hour. *Ring.* It had to be Cait. She had come to her senses. She was sorry. She still loved him. *Ring.* Cait or the five miles? Which would it be?

THE NEXT MORNING a phone message dated the night before arrived on a room-service tray with the shred-ded wheat, skim milk and herbal tea Adam had or-dered for breakfast.

> Called again, but you were out. Forgot to tell you old Lulubell calved again day before last. Petti-est little heifer you ever saw.
>
>   Love,
>   Mom

THAT SAME MORNING a phone message dated the night before arrived on the room-service tray bearing the bittersweet-chocolate croissant and the pot of hot chocolate Cait had ordered for breakfast.

I saw you on *Bite*, and it was love at first sight. If you're not married and would like to be, here's my phone number.

> All my love forever,
> Bruce

Cait blinked at the message through pink-marshmallow eyes. Another cookbook groupie. She blinked again, this time to hold back yet another tear. So much for intuition.

11

By LUNCHTIME on Thursday in Pittsburgh, Cait knew she had to make a decision and make it fast. She might even have to take the biggest risk of her life. A life without Adam in it was infinitely worse than a day without chocolate. Even in the breathless midst of her first book tour she missed him as she might have missed an arm or a leg had it been severed from her.

Perched on a stool at the counter of a coffee shop just around the corner from the bookstore where she'd spent two hours autographing copies of her book, she stared morosely at the untouched chocolate doughnut and cup of hot mocha in front of her.

It was an unprecedented moment. She wasn't hungry at all. Not even for a doughnut. She whose philosophy had always been, "When in doubt, dunk it." Even the Belgian chocolates hadn't eased the pain the night before as they were supposed to. Awful.

Worse than awful, it was serious. Unbelievable as it was, Adam Webster was winning hands down over chocolate. From the fit of her clothes this morning, she figured she had lost another five pounds. With him or without him she was losing.

Cait sighed helplessly at the thought, took a listless bite of the doughnut and forced herself to chew. At this rate she'd waste away to a skeleton before Thanksgiving. But even if she made it to that day intact, what would there be to give thanks for? Before everything fell apart, she had planned on taking Adam home for the holiday to meet her folks.

She forced the doughnut to her lips again but was unable to even take a bite. Dropping it back onto its plate, she pulled an ashtray over and rummaged in her handbag for a cigarette. Somehow she had to get through the rest of the day.

Once lit, though, the thing was as tasteless as the doughnut had been. Wrinkling her nose, Cait stubbed it out after the first puff. She watched it lie bent and dead in the ashtray for a long moment. Then, squaring her shoulders with sudden decision, she plucked it back, wrapped it in a napkin and stowed it in her handbag.

In her rush to get out the door she almost forgot to ask the cashier where the nearest post office was.

IF IT WAS THURSDAY, Adam told himself with weary resignation, this had to be Chicago. The icy wind that whipped his parka collar around his ears would have attested to the fact even if the day of the week hadn't.

Beneath his sneakered feet, the downtown sidewalk was wet with melted sleet from the storm that had blown itself out just in time to give Adam and other Windy City lunchgoers a break.

He shivered and shifted from one foot to the other as he stood in front of a candy store and stared at the sumptuous display of chocolates in the window. Having Cait back, he thought, might be worth looking the other way whenever she indulged in her favorite poison. Hell, he'd bitten his tongue about it until just days ago, hadn't he?

Wouldn't easing this aching loneliness be worth almost anything? He let out a heavy sigh and shook his head in sad denial. Anything but watching her smoke a cigarette a day. There he drew the line. If only she would see reason about that, he might be able to see his way clear to ... to what?

Had he really thought he could commit himself to a woman so cavalier about her own health? But wasn't that question rhetorical? Hadn't he known what she was from the start and fallen headlong in love with her, anyway? And hadn't loving her been as good as life ever got for a guy? You bet it had.

Now, without her, he felt as if he'd been kicked in the gut permanently. He didn't even feel much like running anymore. Last night in Kansas City he'd barely logged a mile.

He dug his chilled hands deeper into his parka pockets and stared hard at the display. Since nothing else had worked, maybe it was time he put himself in her position for a change. After a moment of deep contemplation he straightened his hunched shoulders. What the hell, he told himself as he strode into the shop. What more did he have to lose?

FROM THE POST OFFICE Cait went straight to a telephone booth and rang Jeremy Ainsley.

"Jer, what can you do about switching Boston and Philadelphia so I can do Philadelphia tomorrow morning and Boston in the afternoon? What I'm desperate for is a cooking slot on *Boston Before Dark*."

"Is it a matter of life or death?" Jeremy asked.

"Love or death, Jer."

ON THE SET of *Boston Before Dark* the next day Cait lined her French chef's knife up with careful precision alongside a wire whisk, a chocolate grater and a long, shallow cake pan. On a slow burner to the side butter melted in a small saucepan.

Cait bit her lip and scanned her recipe. Chocolate. Eggs. Sugar. Butter. She was set. Not a thing to worry about—except the most important thing of all.

Pressing her perspiring palms against the burgundy linen apron that protected her lavender silk dress, she glanced around the studio. With just minutes to go before air time, the place was abuzz with activity. There was no studio audience on this show, just a group of college students majoring in electronic media, there to observe the mechanics of airing the program.

Cait craned her neck to see over the milling heads of the students. Then she saw him. He wore a suit, a blue sweat suit as blue as his eyes were green.

Just inside the doorway at the very rear of the studio he stood, as if he had halted there in midstride. Over the heads of the students and studio crew, his piercing green gaze met hers and locked onto it.

Cait brought a clammy hand to her constricted throat. This was *it*. Exactly as she had arranged it. Within the next few seconds she would know whether to give thanks at Thanksgiving or not.

"Look. It's Adam Webster," someone said loudly enough to send heads turning his way. Several students made a move toward him, but he held up a hand to block the rush before it started.

"After the show," Cait heard him say in a tone of quiet, effective command.

He started toward her then, his stride purposeful, his dark-lashed eyes fixed on his destination. Cait couldn't breathe, couldn't think, couldn't move. His expression revealed nothing she could interpret.

Then suddenly he was behind the counter, beside her, lifting her typewritten recipe from the counter.

"Chocolate Ribbon Torte," he read. "Looks like a, er, a real winner, if you ask me."

Cait's hand at her throat went limp as air filled her lungs and her mind sprang back from paralysis. She searched his face with her eyes.

"You got it—the package I sent by overnight mail?"

His mouth curved in a slow grin. "Nothing like one cigarette in the morning to wake a man up."

"I meant what I wrote in the note," Cait murmured, her heart thrumming with sudden joy. "Chocolate stays, but that smoke was my last."

"I know it was, sweet. But I'd have been back even if it wasn't. The last few days have been hell. Come here, Cait. I can't go one more second without a taste of you. Talk about addictions."

He gathered her into his arms, and Cait molded her body to his, lifted her lips to his kiss. Dimly, above the roar of her heart in her ears, Cait heard a wolf whistle from one of the assembled students, then another, followed by loud applause.

"Adam," she mumbled against his lips, "we have an audience that won't stop."

"Yeah, they're worse than the M&M&Ms at breaking up a love scene," Adam mumbled back. He kissed her once more, deeply and thoroughly, and then held her a little away from him. "Before the cameras roll, tell me just one thing."

"Anything."

"Why are you still in Boston when you were supposed to be here this morning and gone by now?"

"I switched schedules. I knew you'd be on this show and . . . well, I had to see you."

"Have you been back to your hotel today?"

"Back? I haven't even checked in yet. My bags went ahead while I rushed to an autograph session and then over here."

"Then you haven't seen the box I expressed to you from Chicago."

"Box of what?"

"Oh, just a few buttercreams, nougats, caramels, cordials, divinities and a half dozen of those things they call truffles with a *T*."

Cait's eyes misted with sudden, loving tears. "Oh, Adam Webster. You do know the way to my heart."

"Like you know every step of the way to mine, such as it is. By the way, sweet, when do we step together down the aisle?"

"You mean . . . ?"

"Will you marry me, sweet?"

"Yes, yes and yes again."

"Hey, what happened to Cautious Cait?"

"Never heard of her. What is this, Adam, *Twenty Questions*?"

"Only one more, I promise. Do we want the wedding cake to be chocolate or chocolate?"

"Hmm, why don't we decide that together on our next bike ride."

"Three minutes to air time!" came the call.

Harlequin Temptation dares to be different!

Once in a while, we Temptation editors spot a romance that's truly innovative. To make sure *you* don't miss any one of these outstanding selections, we'll mark them for you.

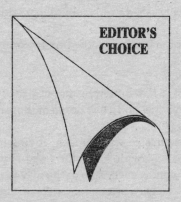

EDITOR'S CHOICE

When the "Editors' Choice" fold-back appears on a Temptation cover, you'll know we've found that extra-special page-turner!

THE *Temptation* EDITORS

You'll flip . . . your pages won't!
Read paperbacks *hands-free* with

Book Mate • I

The perfect "mate" for all your romance paperbacks

**Traveling • Vacationing • At Work • In Bed • Studying
• Cooking • Eating**

Perfect size for all standard paperbacks, this wonderful invention makes reading a pure pleasure! Ingenious design holds paperback books OPEN and FLAT so even wind can't ruffle pages – leaves your hands free to do other things. Reinforced, wipe-clean vinyl-covered holder flexes to let you turn pages without undoing the strap . . . supports paperbacks so well, they have the strength of hardcovers!

Pages turn WITHOUT opening the strap.

SEE-THROUGH STRAP

Reinforced back stays flat.

Built in bookmark.

BOOK MARK

BACK COVER HOLDING STRIP

10" x 7¼", opened.
Snaps closed for easy carrying, too.

Available now. Send your name, address, and zip code, along with a check or money order for just $5.95 + .75¢ for postage & handling (for a total of $6.70) payable to Reader Service to:

Reader Service
Bookmate Offer
901 Fuhrmann Blvd.
P.O. Box 1396
Buffalo, N.Y. 14269-1396

Offer not available in Canada
* New York and Iowa residents add appropriate sales tax.

BM-G

COMING NEXT MONTH